Braless in
WONDERLAND

Braless (in) WONDERLAND

DEBBIE REED FISCHER

Dutton Books

DUTTON BOOKS
A member of Penguin Group (USA) Inc.
Published by the Penguin Group
Penguin Group (USA) Inc., 375 Hudson Street, New York, New York 10014, U.S.A.
Penguin Group (Canada), 90 Eglinton Avenue East, Suite 700, Toronto, Ontario, Canada
M4P 2Y3 (a division of Pearson Penguin Canada Inc.) • Penguin Books Ltd, 80 Strand, London
WC2R 0RL, England • Penguin Ireland, 25 St Stephen's Green, Dublin 2, Ireland
(a division of Penguin Books Ltd) • Penguin Group (Australia), 250 Camberwell Road,
Camberwell, Victoria 3124, Australia (a division of Pearson Australia Group Pty Ltd)
Penguin Books India Pvt Ltd, 11 Community Centre, Panchsheel Park, New Delhi - 110 017, India
Penguin Group (NZ), 67 Apollo Drive, Rosedale, North Shore 0632, New Zealand
(a division of Pearson New Zealand Ltd) • Penguin Books (South Africa) (Pty) Ltd,
24 Sturdee Avenue, Rosebank, Johannesburg 2196, South Africa
Penguin Books Ltd, Registered Offices: 80 Strand, London WC2R 0RL, England

CIP Data is available.

Published in the United States by Dutton Books,
a member of Penguin Group (USA) Inc.
345 Hudson Street, New York, New York 10014
www.penguin.com/youngreaders

Designed by Liz Frances

Printed in USA First Edition

ISBN 978-0-525-47954-3

1 3 5 7 9 10 8 6 4 2

*For my husband, Eric, the love of my life,
who always believed I'd get published and
who generously supported me in every possible way.
I couldn't have done it without you.*

"I know who I was when I got up this morning, but I think I must have been changed several times since then."

—Lewis Carroll,
Alice in Wonderland

STOP

If you're reading this and expecting a tale of some top model who wins the heart of a rock star, adopts a third world baby, launches her own clothing line, winds up on the cover of *Us Weekly*'s Who's Hot issue, and gets her own reality show (or at least, her own *E! True Hollywood Story*), then I better warn you. . . . That's not exactly what happened to me.

Okay, yes, I *was* the It Model on South Beach for about a minute. But if you want to know the truth, I'm not even that hot, really. I look amazing in photos, but the astonishing fact is, I'm not exactly a goddess in person with my thin lips and ordinary nose. Although I do have great teeth and shiny, swingy brown hair. I didn't say I was a bow-wow. But I'm definitely more of the cute-and-sweet-but-not-a-threat kind than the so-smokin'-you-better-stay-away-from-my-boyfriend kind.

So it would blow your mind if you saw the pictures in my portfolio. Who knew that I, Allee Rosen, random citizen of Cape Comet, Florida, high school senior and Wal-Mart employee of the month, could photograph so well? Not me. And I never, *ever* wanted to be a model, that's for sure. I just kinda fell into it, like Alice down the rabbit hole.

And now here I am, getting out of Wonderland, cruising down Fifth Street with the top down in my old red Beetle convertible. Three months ago, I would have been driving past RVs full of models and photography production teams. Or I might have been in one of those RVs, booked for a job. But now modeling season is over and there isn't an RV in sight. Like me, most people in the industry are headed somewhere else, moving on.

A banner-toting plane flies above, reading DJ GALAXAFUNK TONIGHT AT MANSION. A bus passes me with the sign TOO JAYS. WE BRAKE FOR PASTRAMI ON RYE. I'm leaving a city of blurred lines between old and new, where people and buildings reinvent themselves but stay the same, where work is fun and fun is work.

I pick up speed going under the MACARTHUR CAUSEWAY sign, getting to my favorite part of the drive. To my right, I can see sailboats and yachts sailing around Star Island, and to my left, cruise ships as big as skyscrapers float in the bay. I wish I could stay in Miami Beach and soak up this view forever, but I've gotta keep moving, right past this exit sign for BISCAYNE BOULEVARD.

I'm bummed to leave, even though there were times it was rough being here. Especially at first, when Brynn was so hard on me. I wonder if I'll ever see her again, and if she'll ever get help. I have a feeling I'll see Summer again, though, on the big screen. As for Claudette, she'll keep in touch while she travels the world, living her adventure.

And Miguel. Just thinking about that funny, sweet little guy makes me smile. He brought out a side of me I didn't even know was there. He's the friend I'll miss the most.

The exit signs are just up ahead, splitting the road into different directions. 836 WEST AIRPORT takes me away and I-95 NORTH keeps me back home.

I know where I'm going now. After weighing all the pros and cons, I'm not torn about which direction to take anymore. Okay, maybe, a little. But I know I'm doing what's right for me. This morning, I sent the letter, so now my decision is official.

It was a hard decision to make and not everyone likes my choice, but I've learned that I'm the only one who has to like my choices, because I'm the only one who has to live with them. And that's one thing modeling has taught me.

Although back when I started, I didn't think modeling had anything to teach me. In fact, the day the flyer about the model search was floating around school, causing a big squeal-a-baloo with all the Trendy Wendies, I was too busy stealing toilet paper to even notice.

chapter ① ɔʜɒdʇǝɿ

I was on my knees in the handicapped stall (they always have extra TP in there), trying to squish one last roll into my backpack. My backpack was pretty big, so I could fit a lot in if I carried my books. Some girls were primping in front of the mirror, looking at me like I was cuckoo for Cocoa Puffs, but I stayed focused on my mission until I heard, "What are you doing?"

It was Hillary High Beams. In a halter top with no bra. Her chest was like a man's crotch in spandex bike shorts. You knew you should look away, but it was hard not to be curious. "Allee, do you have a problem or something, 'cause I have Tums in my purse if you need it."

I looked up at her, forcing my eyes to stay on her face. "Hillary, if you keep Tums in your purse, aren't you the one with the problem?"

"No," she said, all defensive. "I'm just kidding. Can't you take a joke?"

"Sorry," I said, and plunked my backpack on the sink counter, struggling with the zipper. "I'm a little stressed out right now. This zipper won't close."

She tried to peek inside my backpack. "What *are* you doing with all that toilet paper anyway?"

"Using it for an art project I have to finish next period. It's due today. We're supposed to use a household item."

"So . . . you don't have toilet paper at home?"

I gave her my best deadpan. "No. We don't."

Her eyes widened. "Really?"

Omigod, now who couldn't take a joke? "Yeah, we do, but not enough, and I didn't have time to buy more." I didn't feel like explaining that my four-year-old brother, Robby, had decided that all that extra Charmin I'd brought back from my late shift at Wal-Mart belonged in the bathtub with him. He was such a pain, but so cute.

"You should smile more, Allee. It changes your whole face, you know? You're always so, like, Queen Serious."

Was I smiling? I hadn't realized it. And so what if I was Queen Serious lately? You try smiling when your college plans have been ripped apart like a movie ticket. I should have said, "At least people look at my face, Hill-o-boobs!" That's what I should have said. Instead I said, "Oh. Good to know."

I really had to work on being more assertive.

"So, why'd you come to school yesterday?" she asked. "Every-

7

body knows you were here. Did you forget it was Senior Skip Day or what?"

Why did she care? It's not like we ran in the same circles. Although I didn't really run in any circles. "I had a Spanish test review."

"That is so lame. Where's your senioritis? You should be partying." She wagged an acrylic-nailed finger at me. "Even a Jane Brain like you needs to chill once in a while."

Now it was my turn to get defensive. "I chill once in a while." It just depended on what you meant by chill. Hillary chilled by guzzling beer bongs and freak dancing with football players, whereas my fave mode of chilling involved MTV2, a Jane Austen novel, and Oreos dipped in milk. I kinda chilled by myself. Although she would have been shocked to know that I did shed my punk and alternative tunes and put on some Beyoncé for a little hip-hop dancing action sometimes. Not that I'd ever danced in public. I didn't fly my freak flag out in the open. Maybe because my sister, Sabrina, once caught me in our room and said Shakira is wrong, my hips do lie, 'cause they look like they're dodging bullets, not dancing.

I didn't feel much like dancing these days, though, not since my dream of going to Yale had crumbled like a milk-soaked Oreo. See, my dad dropped a nuke on me, right after Yale's early-acceptance packet came in the mail. It turned out his plan to "increase" my college fund hadn't turned out the way it was supposed to. As soon as he said, "You know, sweetheart, investments aren't always a sure thing," I knew. And I was devastated. How could my dad screw up so royally?

I'd always wanted to go there, ever since Mrs. Anderson, my

ninth-grade English teacher, planted that seed of ambition in me. She'd gone to Yale and was always talking about how much it changed her life, how amazing her professors were, how she still kept in touch with all her Yale friends. Mrs. Anderson told me I could go there too, if I wanted. I just had to keep my eye on the prize.

And I got in. The thing is, I'm not spooky brilliant like Sanjay Singh, who has a photographic memory and thinks calculus is easy. I mean, sure, I was in AP classes and gifted and all that stuff, but I knew the score. I got in because I worked my butt off, not because I was some Einstein.

But all that work was for nothing now. I couldn't even get financial aid. If the world were fair, aerospace engineers like my dad would make millions, but in reality-ville, my parents made just enough so that I didn't qualify for aid, but not enough to be able to pay for a private college. So, according to Yale, we were too rich to need financial help. Never mind that we were too poor to pay full tuition. I could have gotten a loan, but then I'd have a mountain of debt to pay off for the next thirty years, and what if I couldn't pay it back? There was some state scholarship money I'd won, and I still had money left in my college fund, just not *quite* enough. My $6.67 an hour at Wal-Mart wasn't exactly piling up at the bank, either.

So that was it. Yale wasn't in the cards. I had to accept it.

Except I couldn't. Call it denial if you want, but I still had this crazy hope there was a way to get there. I just needed to figure out how.

"Well, you missed an awesome party at the beach yesterday," Hillary said.

"Yeah! It rocked!" some girl shouted from inside a stall.

9

"I know." I sighed. "I heard all about it." From Sabrina, the only freshman invited to Senior Skip Day, thanks to a bunch of drooling senior guys.

There! Zipper closed. Mission accomplished. I threw on my super-bulky backpack and headed out of the bathroom, joining the flow of kids in the hallway. Mysteriously, Hillary followed me. "Have you seen Sabrina anywhere?" she asked.

"No." Everybody was always looking for The Fluff. That's what I secretly called her in my mind because she was your basic cloud of cotton candy: all fluff, no stuff. I was more like a hundred percent whole wheat, solid and full of fiber. How we both sprang from our parents' loins was one of the great unexplained wonders of the world. "Have you checked the breezeway?"

"Uh-uh. I was just wondering, um, is she going to the model search this Saturday? Do you know if she heard about it?"

"What model search?"

"This one." She whipped out a flyer from her jeans pocket and unfolded it in front of my face. *Attention all beautiful people! Do you have what it takes to be a fashion model? International Scouting Associates, America's most successful modeling scouts, are coming to your area looking for new, fresh faces. We have placed models with the world's most exclusive agencies, such as Elite and Ford. Come to Cocoa Square Mall this Saturday, January 5, at ten a.m. Bring a full-face photo and full-body photo and get a free beauty evaluation. Come and get discovered!*

A beauty evaluation? Excuse me. I felt barf rising. "No, I haven't heard her say anything about this."

"You're sure?" Jake and Scott slinked by, ogling Hillary's high beams. Gross. Those two were partners in slime. They couldn't

10

even pass the Georgia O'Keeffe poster in the art room without making a dirty joke. I mean, maybe her flowers *did* look like a certain part of the female anatomy, but grow up, ya pervs. "Sabrina doesn't know *anything* about the model search?"

"Yeah, I'm sure. If she's going, I would've heard about it by now. That's weird, though, 'cause she's always talking about wanting to be a model. But no, she hasn't said anything to me."

She looked relieved. I guess she was worried my sister would steal her glory. I understood why she was threatened. Most girls were, with The Fluff's violet blue eyes and compact perfect body. Even I would be lying if I said I'd never felt an occasional twinge of jealousy. I'd just learned to blow it off and remember that I had better hair.

Because here was the cold truth about two sisters at the same school: one of them was always prettier. And people had a way of reminding you who's who. Kinda like right now.

"Um, Allee, could you do me a favor?" she asked.

"Sure." So *that's* why she was following me. She probably wanted my review notes from Spanish. Why should I do her a favor when I barely knew her? Girls like her were just so used to everyone doing them favors. They expected it. It's how they got through life.

She waved the flyer around. "About the model search, could you just forget to mention it to Sabrina? Like, don't tell her at all, okay?" She glanced behind me at my backpack. "Uh-oh, it's coming open."

"What's coming open?"

"The zipper. Wait, I can fix it." Now she was fumbling with my backpack.

"Don't! They'll all—"

Fall out. And they did, one after the other, unraveling, streaming down the arts wing, carpeting the hallway. This was a disaster. How was I going to finish my project now? Some comedian shouted, "Hey, look, you're on a roll!" Then people started tossing pieces in the air, throwing entire rolls around like a game of hot potato. Hillary joined them. They all seemed so relaxed, so happy. I was the only one not smiling or laughing. I wished I could, I really did. But I didn't have it in me. None of this was funny to me.

My life was unraveling, just like this toilet paper.

Smack. A roll hit me square in the forehead. It got me so irritated I picked the roll up off the floor and chucked it. It hit Hillary. Right in the butt. She threw it back, but I caught it, just as a stray piece floated down and landed on my head, covering my face.

Which is why I didn't see the next roll coming. It got me good. Right in the ear.

And then a weird thing happened, even weirder than seeing the hallway carpeted in toilet paper. This time, instead of getting irritated, I got . . . the giggles. Waves and waves of them. The next thing I knew, I was cracking up, throwing the stuff around with the others. Forget my project. So what if I was about to get the first F of my life? Hilarious! Maybe this was senioritis. Maybe I'd finally caught it from everybody else.

All I knew was, I hadn't laughed like this in a long time.

And it felt good.

chapter ②

I didn't mean to spit it all in her face. It just happened. I seriously meant to swallow it, but when The Fluff announced she was going to be the next big supermodel and made that ridiculous face, it was like, *thar she blows*.

It happened at dinner. Mom made the most delish *arroz con pollo*, chicken with rice. We ate Cuban or Jewish food most of the time because Dad is Jewish and Mom is Cuban-American. We called it Jewban cuisine. But tonight Mom put something American on the menu.

Pea soup.

So there we were, eating it and talking about Hillary High Beams, who, by the way, was wasting her time trying to silence me because the whole school had found out about the model search today, including my sister. There were flyers all over the place. Joey DiSalvo, our student council prez, ended his daily intercom announcements with, "For those of you who want information on the modeling thing at the mall, extra flyers will be available at my dad's place." DiSalvo's Bait, Tackle, and Pizza is the nucleus of Cape Comet. Our tiny town was near the Kennedy Space Center and the Air Force base, and whether you were military, techie, or townie, every weekend you'd wind up at DiSalvo's for a slice and maybe some new rubber worms.

Anyway, I was telling my sister that Hillary should start wearing a bra. "I'm all for freedom and comfort," I said. "But bouncing around like that is demeaning to all women."

"I bounce too," Robby said. "I jump on my bed."

"I don't know about it being demeaning," The Fluff said. "But it's not a good look for her. I mean, hello, who wears a backless halter top with a D cup? Hillary's so fashion backward. Although . . ." She paused to raise her spoon thoughtfully. "She *was* the first to put rhinestones on her drill team uniform, and that looked hot."

"Everyone talks about that girl at all the PTA meetings," Mom said. "I don't know how her mother lets her run around like that. Tight shirt, no bra, and those tiny miniskirts she barely fits into. I'd be so embarrassed if that was my daughter."

"Allee, did you get a chance to look at those college brochures I left on your bed?" Dad asked. I shook my head no. "Are you going to?" I shrugged. I hadn't been talking to him much lately. I knew he hadn't blown my Yale fund on purpose. I knew I shouldn't blame him. But it was hard not to. My sister's eyes met mine. She knew what I was thinking.

Dad tried again. "Because you've already missed some application deadlines." He kept looking at me through his glasses, silently begging me to answer him, like a puppy hoping for a biscuit.

And so I caved. "I'll look at them later, Dad."

"Does anybody want more soup before I serve the chicken?" Mom asked.

"I would, but it's too salty," said Abuela. My grandmother. She lived with us. There were two things we tuned out in our house: 1) the constant roar of planes flying overhead from the base, and 2) Abuela.

"Sabrina, you've barely touched your soup," Mom said. "Eat."

"I can't. I need a flat stomach for the model audition tomorrow."

Abuela adjusted her wig and said, "I could have been a fashion model in my youth." *I kood ha-beeng a fachon model een my jooth.* Abuela was always announcing what she could have been. So far, according to her, she could have been a famous actress, a millionaire's wife, a dancer, an opera singer, and a professional harmonica player. From what I saw, she could have been a professional TV watcher.

"Hey, Mom, did you TiVo that *Oprah* for me?" I asked her. "The one with that lady who wrote *The Vagina Monologues*?"

"You said the F word." Robby giggled. "Fa-China!"

Mom slapped her forehead. "I'm so sorry, Allee. I forgot. But I did TiVo the *Oprah* with all the beauty secrets." Just another example of how Mom did not understand me at all. Like I cared about eyebrow plucking or preventing wrinkles or whatever. I was way more interested in feminists, always had been, ever since I'd learned about the suffragettes in sixth grade. I even dressed up as Susan B. Anthony for Halloween that year, but none of the neighbors got it. They thought I was Mrs. Butterworth.

Mom didn't even need to watch a show about beauty secrets. Her friends were always oohing and aahing about how young she looked and how she could pass for Catherine Zeta-Jones. "Watch the *Oprah* I taped anyway, honey," Mom said to me. "You might learn something. Like how to keep your ponytail from getting so messy."

I groaned. "I'm not gonna watch a show telling me how I'm *supposed* to look. Shows like that are the reason women can't just be happy with themselves," I told her. "Same with magazines."

"Lighten up, Wednesday Addams, it was just a suggestion," Mom answered. I used to get really insulted whenever she called me that, but then I found out Wednesday Addams was this really smart, wiseass goth kid from an old seventies show. Now I had a WHAT WOULD WEDNESDAY ADDAMS DO? bumper sticker that I'd custom made for my car. Mom went on with her usual lecture. "And you may not like it, Allee, but everyone is judged by their appearance. The way you look says a lot about you. That's why I wish you'd give up those faded old jeans of yours with the rip in the knee. Do you want people saying you're a slob?"

"No, I've got you to do that for me." God, Mom cared so much what other people thought.

"I don't call you a slob. I just want you to look your best, that's all."

"I like those jeans," said The Fluff. "But rips are so over. You can*not* wear those, Allee." Then she suddenly gasped, "Omigod!"

"What?" we all asked, alarmed.

"I still have to figure out what I'm wearing tomorrow for the model search."

"Omigod, what if you don't figure it out?" I squealed. She rolled her eyes at me. "Those model thingies are always scams," I told her. "It's in a *mall*. How real can it be?"

"In Cuba, they used to write songs about me, I was so beautiful," said Abuela.

"Hillary will probably be my biggest competition," The Fluff said. "Breasts are like, very in right now."

It was at this point my pea soup had a little trouble going down.

"Okay, then I think I'll try out to be a model," I said to her. "I've got the boobage."

"Ha-ha, like you're serious," my sister answered. A second later, her forehead filled up with worry lines. "Are you?" Everyone at the table cracked up. I was the last person who would *ever* be interested in being a model. Hello, I had a brain. "I knew you were joking," she lied.

"You did not," I said. "You're so gullible. Remember when I told you Betty Crocker is a real person?"

"She is a real person, isn't she? I mean, her name is on the box." Hoots of laughter all around. Even Robby giggled and he didn't even get the joke. The Fluff crossed her arms and narrowed one blue eye at me. Just one. Her signal for war. "I heard something about you today," she singsonged at me. "I heard you TP'd the arts wing because McDonald failed your project."

"Impossible," Dad said.

"It's true," The Fluff said, folding her arms. "Our little genius finally got a big, fat F." Why was my sister semi-busting me like this? I withheld information from Mom and Dad to cover for her all the time. And this is how she paid me back? She was lucky I'd never told them about all the parties she went to when they thought she was at the movies, or how many times I'd lied for her when she was on a date, since our overprotective parenting duo had said she wasn't old enough to date yet.

"Is it true, Allee?" Mom asked. "Wasn't art supposed to be your easy A this year?"

I narrowed one eye back at my sister. "For your information, I didn't fail anything. I got an incomplete, and he's letting me turn it in on Monday. So it's not an F. It's more like a delayed A."

Mom pointed her spoon at me. "You got lucky, Allee."

The Fluff kicked the table. "As usual. Well, I'm getting lucky too. Take a good look, everyone, because you're looking at the next supermodel of the world." Then she piled her hair on top of her head, stuck her chin out, and did this pouty thing with her lips.

She looked like a fish sucking on a hose. That was all it took. A monster giggle ignited, just like the one earlier today. The only difference was, this time I had a mouth full of soup. *Whoosh.* The dam broke. Green pea goop all over The Fluff's face, the tablecloth, and some of my dad's arm.

"Look what you did!" The Fluff screamed.

"Again, again, again," Robby chanted. "Sabrina got slimed, Sabrina got slimed."

Dad wiped his arm off without a word, but Mom had enough words for both of them. "Oh, very nice, Allee. That's how you show support for your little sister? Just for that, you can drive her to that modeling audition tomorrow."

18

"No way," I said.

"Yes way. You're taking her."

"I want to go too," said Abuela.

"But the mall's an hour away," I said. "And I have to work tomorrow."

"Then switch shifts with someone," Mom said.

"But Allee can't disappoint her Wal-Mart shoppers," The Fluff said. "How will they ever find the loose screws without her assistance?"

"Shut up!" I snapped. She was always making fun of my job, especially since they'd moved me from health and beauty to hardware. She got up at the ass crack of dawn to blow her hair every morning, but hell would freeze over before she would ever get up early to get her hands dirty and do some actual work. I couldn't wait until she turned sixteen and had to get a job. Spoiled brat.

I had just finished tucking Robby in, after reading five pages of *Alice in Wonderland*. He always came to me after he had a nightmare, maybe because I was always willing to snuggle under his covers with a flashlight and read to him. Now I was back in my room. The Fluff was in her bed next to mine, tossing and turning. She'd be asleep soon, tired out from spending hours on the phone with her Trendy Wendy clique.

I climbed into bed and started to read more of *Alice*. It was probably my favorite book of all time. I loved a lot of nineteenth-century books, but mostly the women writers, like Jane Austen and the Brontë sisters. They wrote about strong female characters with opinions, women who didn't keep quiet and didn't do what was expected of them.

But *Alice in Wonderland* was special to me because it was the first story I really fell in love with. I couldn't get enough of all the crazy characters in *Wonderland*. I must have read it twenty times when I was younger.

Tonight I'd read Robby the beginning, the part with the hedge. I loved the idea that behind something as ordinary as a hedge, there could be a Wonderland hiding. Like, you could really get to an alternate, magical universe if you just stumbled down the right rabbit hole. Robby compared it to how the Teenage Mutant Ninja Turtles have a hidden world in the sewer. Boys.

Most of all, I loved Alice. When I was Robby's age, I wanted to *be* Alice, to just drink something and change, be a different person. Nowadays I wanted to be a different person all the time. Like a person who didn't get called Queen Serious. Or maybe a person who had more of a social life.

Sometimes I hung out with a group of kids from my AP classes, like at lunch in the caf, but I wouldn't say I was close with any of them, not like I was with my best friend, Amy. She'd moved away a year ago. Since she left, I'd kinda been on my own.

Who wouldn't want to be Alice? She was funny and smart, and she got to escape boring real life for great adventures. The Fluff and I talked about getting out of Cape Comet all the time. It was like the sleepiest burg on the planet. We both felt trapped.

"Do you think I have a shot tomorrow?" she asked, propping herself up on her elbow so she could look at me. Her hair was rolled up in these little squishy rollers. "Honest opinion. Like, do I really?"

I could have pulled a sarcastic answer out of my stash, but

her eyes were boring into me all searchingly, plus the fact that she was asking me meant she was over the soup thing and I wanted to keep the peace. "Yeah, you've got a shot. You know you'll be the prettiest one there."

And what did I get in return for my niceness? "Just make sure you don't wear that retarded shirt, the one Amy gave you before she left, with that ugly band, what's-it-called."

"Brainless Wankers. It's from their Excuse Me While I Whip This Out tour."

"Yeah. You can't wear that. If they see you with me, you'll ruin my chances. And could you please turn your light off already? Seriously. It's late."

"Everything okay, girls?" Mom called from the hall. There it was, her nightly check-in.

"Yeah," we both answered. What did she think we were doing in here every night, sneaking in boys and playing strip poker while she and Dad lay in bed watching *Everybody Loves Raymond* reruns? Or did she just think we were still two-year-olds? Honestly, Mom and Dad were such helicopter parents, always hovering over us.

"Turn off your light," The Fluff reminded me.

"Just one more chapter."

"If I have dark circles tomorrow, I'll kill you."

"You won't."

After a few minutes, she said, "I'm sorry I told about your art project."

"Why'd you do it?"

"I don't know. I was pissed about the whole Betty Crocker

21

thing." Her voice was wobbly, as if she was about to cry. "I hate it when you make fun of me."

I thought about that. Teasing was what older sisters did. And she *was* ridiculous. But I didn't realize it bothered her *that* much. "I'm sorry. And I really didn't mean to spit soup in your face."

She giggled. "Who knows, maybe it'll be good for my skin."

chapter ③

The mall was a zoo. There hadn't been this much excitement around here since the county Swamp Cabbage Festival. Every school in the county must have gotten flyers because there were about two hundred kids I didn't recognize. Amazing. All this competition for a job where you exploited yourself and didn't even use your brain.

The long line was clumpy with random groups of people, including my sister and her frosh friends. The biggest clump was in front of the table where the model scouts were sitting. A banner that said INTERNATIONAL SCOUTING ASSOCIATES hung over it, with oversize posters of models propped up behind them.

Why was it that whenever I was at the mall I got this sucky

23

anonymous sensation? Like I was a beige stripe in a rainbow. I usually had a who-the-hell-cares attitude about clothes, which was why I was wearing khaki shorts and a black tank top, but looking around at everyone in cool outfits (except for the troop leader/ soccer mom types in their plastic earrings, Christmas sweaters, and waistband-under-the-armpit mom jeans), I was wishing I had a style, any style. Like that goth girl I saw in Hot Topic wearing an Izod shirt with the alligator all cut up and decapitated with hand-painted drops of blood dripping down. I bet she never felt beige.

The Fluff was moving forward in line. She'd overdone it with the makeup; her face was a different color than her neck. And she was nervous, shifting around, adjusting the straps of her long, flowy dress, shuffling the photos she brought with her. She'd made the dress herself, copied it from one she saw on a celebrity in *CosmoGIRL!* My sister might have been the only student at Comet High who actually learned to sew in Domestic Home Skills (aka Desperate Housewife Skills). It was the highest grade she got last semester, a B+, and the only homework I didn't have to help her with. She would have gotten an A but she didn't follow the pattern on her final project. It was supposed to be a basic T-shirt, and she turned it into a wild halter top with a jeweled neckline.

"Allee!" a voice called from behind me. I turned around. It was John, from my humanities class. "You never called me back last night."

"You called me?"

"Yeah. Sabrina was on the other line. She didn't tell you I called?"

"No. Did you need the list of topics for our papers? They're due Monday."

"No. I, uh, I called because, I know it was last-minute, but uh . . ." His ears were turning red. "I just thought, you know, maybe you didn't have plans. . . . I meant to ask you earlier, but I figured it couldn't hurt to see if you were free. . . ."

Oh. John called to ask me out. On a date. I hadn't been on a date since last year, when I went out with Lance for a few months.

". . . Anyway, I gotta work tonight. But, uh, maybe some other time?"

"Um, sure, that'd be great." He was cute. Why hadn't I ever noticed the brown hair and green eyes combo? I would have totally gone out with him. We talked for a few minutes until he said something about having to get to his job at the Super Saver and took off toward the parking lot.

Wow. I never even knew he was interested.

Although I would have found out sooner if Sabrina had given me the message. But she hadn't. Because she forgot. Because she was too busy blabbing on the phone all night to her little buddies about what to wear for today. Because Sabrina only cared about Sabrina.

How hard was it to remember to give someone a message? I could have gone out with him last night if I'd known about his phone call. Dinner and a movie, probably. Maybe even a full-throttle make-out session. But no, I was holed up in our shoe-box of a room, scrunching up toilet paper into flowers for my art project and researching Neolithic civilizations for my humanities paper.

When I could have been on a date. With John. If my sister had given me the damn message.

I could feel my face getting hot. A knot of anger was twisting my insides.

That selfish, stupid little brat. There she was, near the front of the line, joking around with some guys. One of them would probably ask her out. She got asked out all the time. Not like me.

The knot was spreading, coursing through me. How could she just have *forgotten* to tell me? It wasn't important enough, I guess. *I* wasn't important enough.

One of the guys whispered something in her ear. She pushed him away in a flirty way, smiling up at him.

I was going to kill her.

I didn't even realize I was walking toward her until I bumped into some girl dressed like a Brat doll, knocking her photos to the floor. She shouted "Hey!" as I pushed past her, but I didn't stop. I was fuming more and more with every step. All the people in line were a blur. I shouldered them out of my way, ignoring the whines of "Hey, she's cutting." Finally, I got to her, right at the front of the line. My hands were balled into fists. "Did I get a phone call last night?" I shouted in her face.

She looked at me with horror. "What are you doing here?"

"A phone call. Did I get one?"

She answered through her trophy smile. "I don't know. Can we like, discuss this later?"

I knew we were being watched by the people behind the table, but I didn't care. "I can't believe you! Your dumb friends were so important you couldn't get off the phone for *one second* to tell me John called?"

"Allee—"

"He called to ask me out. *Me,* not *you,* for once. How could you not tell me?"

"Allee, not now," she said, still in stiff-lipped ventriloquist mode.

"How many times have I given you your messages, Sabrina? How many times? I always, *always* give you your freaking messages!"

Her smile was gone. She whispered, "Okay, okay, I'm sorry. I'll make it up to you, just don't do this now." Unbelievable. She was still only thinking of herself. I hoped I'd blown this for her. I really did. It would serve her damn self-centered selfish self right.

I was about to storm off when I heard, "Holy handbag, Toto, we're not in Kansas anymore." A man wearing blue eyeliner and blue-tinted aviator sunglasses perched on his completely bald head was sitting behind the table. He touched the arm of the man sitting next to him. "Jay, look what the wind blew in."

"Hallelujah. It's about time," Jay said. He was African-American, with a platinum blond coif. He smiled up at me. "What's your name, honey?"

Normally if a man had addressed me as "honey" I would have written him off as a sexist Neanderthal, but seeing as this Jay person was, in a sense, one of the girls, the rules didn't apply. Besides, his smile was open and friendly. He looked nice. "Allee," I said.

"I'm Jay."

"She's just my sister," The Fluff said, shouldering me off to the side a little. "I'm Sabrina. Did you see the close-up picture of me?"

"Just a sec, honey." He looked me up and down, then said to Baldie, "This one's got snap, crackle, pop, all right."

"Fo sho," agreed Baldie. "And at least she's not wearing one of those long dresses like all these other girls. Those were like, two years ago in Miami." Did he momentarily forget about The Fluff standing in front of him wearing one? "I can't wait to get out of the boonies."

Shame. Shame on my sister's face, painted in salmon-colored splotches all over her cheeks. And shame on me and my total freak-out explosion, stealing her moment. She really wanted to be chosen. She was too innocent to realize this was all bogus.

My rage was gone now, replaced by something else I could only describe as a blood-is-thicker-than-water, sistah-sistah protective instinct. I wanted to tell Baldie that he didn't know anything, that Sabrina Rosen, aka the fresh frosh, was a trendsetter at our school and an A-list hottie whose butt they should have been kissing. I opened my mouth to tell him all that when Baldie grabbed my arm. "Wait. Don't you have any snaps?"

"Snaps?" I asked.

"Snapshots, as in photos," he answered with clipped precision, the way you speak to a child of the special needs variety. "Where are your pictures?"

"She didn't bring any," The Fluff said, pushing her way in front of me. "It's mine you want to see, remember?" She tapped on the table where her pictures were scattered. "I know the flyer said to bring two, but I thought you'd have a better perspective of how I photograph with more angles."

"Mm-hmm," Jay said to her in the same manner my mother "Mm-hmm"s us when she's pretending she just heard what we said but is really listening to *Oprah*. "Allee, how tall are you?"

"Five eight."

"No, you're not," Baldie said, turning to Jay. "She's a bit more. I'll measure her." He bolted out from behind the table with a measuring tape and got behind me. "Take off your flip-flops. Stand up straight."

I turned around and stared at him. He stared back. These people were rip-off artists. I mean, hello, he was just capitalizing on insecure young women who were looking for validation through their physical appearance. I should have told him that. Although, from what I could see, this guy had such an attitude, I doubted anyone could tell him anything. I'd have probably had better luck explaining feminism to Hugh Pervner and the staff at *Playboy*.

He waved the measuring tape at me and raised his eyebrows. Oh, what the hell, why not let him measure me? I was here. And honestly, I was kinda curious. Although if Baldie thought I was like one of these suckers in line, he had another think coming.

He measured me from top to bottom. "What about Sabrina?" I asked him.

"Yeah, what about me?" she asked with a nervous laugh. "Hello, hi, I'm the one auditioning." They totally ignored her.

"About five eight and three-quarters," Baldie said.

"She's five nine," Jay said. "What about the rest?"

He wrapped the tape around my hips, waist, and chest. There was a sudden hush from the line, which, of course, happened while he was measuring my chestal area. A growth spurt last summer had surpassed my mammary expectations when I spurted from an A to a C. I noticed Hillary from the corner of my eye, chewing on her lip. No worries, Hills. I was no threat to her bodacious territory.

29

"Thirty-five, twenty-four, thirty-five," he said. Flashes went off in my face. Jay was taking pictures with a digital camera. A tingly warmth came over me. These people actually thought I was the prettier one. It was like *Freaky Friday*, only I'd switched places with my sister instead of my mom.

This was so not for real. "Am I being punked?" I asked, glancing around. "Seriously. This is one of those shows, right?"

The Fluff started glancing around. "Yeah, are those sunglasses a hidden camera?"

Jay looked up at her, leaned forward, and quietly told her, "Honey, you're a pretty girl. You might want to try the beauty pageant circuit."

Uh-oh, knife to the heart. My sister thought beauty pageants were the corniest, most degrading things ever. It was one of the few things we agreed upon. I reached for her hand, but she shook it away. "But look how I photograph. Look at my pictures. You'll see—"

"You're not right for our clients. I'm sorry."

"But what if I—"

"You're too short," interrupted Baldie.

"I could do petite modeling."

"You still need to be five seven for petite modeling."

"I'm five seven."

"No, you're not," Baldie said. "You're a little under five six, probably five five and a half." How did he know that? She was exactly five five and a half. She'd made me measure her last night. "And the only thing five five is good for is furniture ads or a magician's assistant."

Jay said, "Forget modeling, Serena. It's not for you. What you should be is an actress/spokesperson. We have a big convention coming up in Las Vegas. Over a hundred talent agents will be there, and the attendance fee is only three hundred dollars. Take a brochure at the end of the table."

Baldie added, "Bit of advice, though, Precious? Lose all that makeup. Keep it fresh. You're not Christina Aguilera. You're trying too hard, so take it down a notch, more like your sister here, know what I'm saying?"

Her lip was quivering. She wouldn't look at me. She scooped up her pictures and took off.

Baldie gave her a little wave. "Best of luck."

I made hard eye contact with Baldie. "I can't believe you didn't give her a chance. She's the prettiest girl here."

"Being pretty and being a model are two different things."

"Yeah, but she wants to be one really badly."

"Precious, nobody chooses modeling. It chooses you."

"Is there someone else who can see us?" some girl whined from down the line.

Jay held up the digital camera. He and Baldie stared at it, commenting.

"Amazing skin. Like caviar and pearls." Wow, my skin was like caviar and pearls?

"Great teeth."

"And hair. It's every color from chocolate to butter."

"She's commercial, not fashion."

"Oh, def. Very commercial."

Jay looked up and snapped another picture of me. "I'm just going to take a couple more. We need a profile, front-on, and full-body." He was waiting for me to do something. I felt silly, but I tossed my hair like I was in a shampoo commercial. "Good, hold it." *Snap.* "Now smile. Chin out." *Snap.* "Shake your hair again. How do you get such fabulous highlights? You must have a great stylist."

Highlights? I got my hair cut once a year. Mom insisted that I do it every December for NASA's annual nondenominational holiday barbecue. I jogged on the beach a lot. That could explain it. "No stylist. It's sun."

"Sun? I've never heard of it. Where can I buy some?" I grinned. *Snap.* "Great teeth, Allee."

"Are your parents here?" Baldie asked.

"No."

"What size shoe are you?"

"Ten."

"Good. You'll be five ten in no time. How old are you?"

"Sixteen. I'll be seventeen next month. I skipped first grade, so I'm younger than—"

"Great smiling shots. Momma will love her. In fact, let's send these to Momma today."

Momma? Who the hell was Momma? A pistol-packing, cowboy-hat-wearing tobacco-spitter came to mind. Actually, who cared who Momma was? None of this was legit. By this time next week I'd probably have a steaming pile of junk mail from cheesy modeling schools.

The Fluff was waiting for me on a bench by the entrance, looking extremely pissed off. When I started walking toward her, she shot me an angry look, got up, and stomped out the door, without looking back.

chapter ④

Right now my life was more drama-packed than a Telemundo soap. First there was the Abuela problem. Last weekend we were finishing our usual Sunday dinner of DiSalvo's pizza when Abuela came home from some funeral, sniffing and waving a lace hankie around. Maybe she really could have been an actress, because I happened to know she couldn't stand the lady who died. And she kept going on and on about how she's so much more golden than all the other golden girls who were there. ". . . Ana used to walk around like she was the last Coca-Cola in the desert, and look at her now, in a wheelchair, and she's younger than me. I could salsa all night long, I could do a hundred jumping jacks (*yumping yacks*), cook a ten-course gourmet meal, sing an aria . . ." and blah-blapity-blah-blah. For someone who sat around in a recliner glued to the TV all day, she was really wasting all her talents. Anyway, none of us were paying attention until she said, "I met a nice man at the wake. A *very* nice man."

Dad snorted. "A man? At your age, Maria?"

"What, you think I'm a dinosaur?"

"Yeah, you're a pterodactyl! You're a pterodactyl!" Robby shouted. Did I mention he was a dino-holic? It was obsessive. He'd been wearing the same stinky dinosaur socks for four days.

Abuela ignored him and widened her mascara-encrusted eyes as if a horde of TV cameras were zooming in on her for a close-up. "Well, you'll never believe this." She stopped for a theatrical pause, then said, "He's getting me a *yob.*" It took me a full five seconds to realize she was referring to employment, and I was still recovering from that info when she cried, "At Wal-Mart! Allee, *mi vida*, we'll be working together!" I didn't know what she said after that due to the inner shriek of hysteria echoing through my brain.

The man was Artie Kovic, a greeter who'd been there forever. So now, for the past week, Abuela had been "working," which meant she was sitting next to Artie, watching him hand out carts and stickers. What sucked the most was that Wal-Mart kindly matched our shifts, so now I was stuck driving Miss Lazy.

The Fluff was loving it all. Whenever Abuela and I left the house in our matching blue vests, she went, "Gee, I didn't know polyester was in this season," or "Are those from Wal-Mart's ready-to-wear collection?" And that was about all she'd said to me in a week. She hadn't even asked me to help her with any homework. I actually missed helping her too. She just couldn't get over

34

the fact that I'd stolen her spotlight for once, even though I hadn't meant to.

And then there was Robby, getting out of his bed and crawling into mine every night. He was too afraid to go downstairs to Mom and Dad's bedroom so he came to me, all trembling and clutching his giant T. rex, freaked out from a bad dream. It wouldn't have been so bad if he hadn't had that little bed-wetting problem.

On top of everything, something was up with my parents. They were really quiet lately. Sometimes Dad looked like one of those cigar-store Indians, arms crossed, lips pursed, Chief No Talk. I heard them talking sometimes, in the kitchen usually, but whenever I walked in, they'd stop. They had some big secret. Oh, God. I hoped Mom wasn't preggo again (*ew, disturbing visual, deny, deny, deny*). Another kid. That was all this family needed. It was crowded enough around here.

I swear, between my parents' secret conversations, my sister giving me the cold shoulder, Robby in my bed, Abuela in my car and at my job, no clue where I was going to college, and graduation in front of me like a brick wall, I was suffocating. The words *Ican'tbreatheIcan'tbreatheIcan'tbreathe* chugged through my thoughts like a train sometimes. The other night I went running at ten o'clock just to get my ya-yas out.

I wished I could wake up and be someone else.

We'd all been called into the family room, even Robby and Abuela. Mom and Dad were sitting on the couch. "There's something Mom and I need to discuss with you all," Dad said. My sister bit her lower lip and gave me this look. It was the same look she used to give me during a scary movie when she wanted me to hold her hand, or when a bad storm rattled our bedroom windows and she wanted me to hide in the closet with her. I got up from the ottoman, stepped over Robby rolling around on the floor with his T. rex, and sat next to her on the love seat. Her eyes thanked me. Maybe after this meeting we could finally talk.

Mom took a deep breath, blew it out slowly, and looked at me. "Remember that day you went to see those model scouts at the mall?"

The Fluff brightened. "Did they call?"

"Yes, they did. They've called a few times."

My sister bounced forward. "What did they say? Did they change their minds about me? Do they want me?"

Mom bit her lip, not answering. She turned to Dad, who said, "They said you were very pretty but that you need to grow some more. You can try again in a few years, sweetheart." Dad cleared his throat. "Actually, Allee, it's you they're interested in. The scouts showed this agency your pictures, and apparently they— this agency—would like to meet you."

Huh?

My parents were waiting for me to say something, but what was I supposed to say? None of this modeling stuff was true. It couldn't be. I was afraid to look at my sister. She was the only one with a response: *"OOWWHAAAT?"*

Mom answered calmly, as if my sister hadn't just shrieked like a crazy mofo. "I know this isn't what you expected, Sabrina, and I'm so sorry, sweetheart, really I am."

"I'm sorry too, honey," Dad said. "Sometimes things don't

work out the way we planned." His eyes came back to mine. "The agent's name is Momma, if you can believe that."

Momma? I rewound Baldie's last words: *Let's send these to Momma today.*

Oh, for God's sake.

They had to be kidding me.

My poor, naive parents actually thought those model scouts were legit. Me and modeling? They honestly thought someone in Miami wanted *me* to sign a modeling contract? HA! Psychotic breaks, anyone? They'd totally lost their grip on reality.

"*Perdón,*" Abuela said. "But why do they want to see Allee? I mean, Allee, *mi vida,* you're a genius like your father, but no offense . . ." I braced myself. Abuela always said "no offense" right before she said something really offensive. "You're no great beauty, not like I was at your age. Sabrina's the one who should be a model, not you."

"*Mamá, por favor!*" Mom shouted, throwing her hands up.

"Exactly!" said The Fluff. "Abuela is right. Allee is *not* model material. Look at her." My whole family scanned me up and down with these puzzled expressions. It was not a good feeling.

"Well, the experts think she is," said Mom, scratching her head. "They think she's beautiful and a good type for commercials and catalogs." I looked at myself in the mirror across from me, hanging above the couch, trying to see what it was those modeling people saw.

"Allee doesn't know the first thing about the fashion industry!" my sister shouted. "*I* do. And which agency is this, anyway?"

"Finesse," Dad said. "Ever heard of them?"

"Finesse? *Finesse?* Of course I've heard of them. There's no way they want Allee. This is bull!"

"Calm down, Sabrina," Mom said. "You'll have another chance someday."

But she was winding up. "How'd they get our number anyway? She didn't even fill out an application at the mall."

"No, but you did," Dad said. "And you told them you were sisters."

"It's not fair!" She stood up and threw a couch pillow at my face, but I caught it. Perfectly. Which led her to this explosion: "Everything always has to be about you, doesn't it, Allee? Miss Overachiever. You know what you're number one at? Being the worst sister in the entire world! I'll never forgive you for stealing this from me! I hate you!" She ran out and stomped up the stairs, then came back down and pointed at me like she was about to deliver a gypsy curse. "Just wait. You think you know everything, but you don't know anything. You'll see." Then she was gone again.

What did *I* do? Tears stung my eyes.

Mom said the same thing to me that Jay had said at the mall. "Don't worry, Allee, she'll get over it." Dad nodded, agreeing.

Abuela got up and started shuffling out, probably to try to calm my sister down. Or maybe it was just time for her favorite show, *El Gordo y la Flaca.* "Robby," she said, " *ven conmigo.* Let's go upstairs. I have gummi bears in my room." They both went upstairs.

"So what do you think, Allee?" Dad asked. "Do you want to be a model?" He sounded like an infomercial. *Do you want to be a real estate ace? A professional in the medical field? A hip-hop dancer?* "Should we drive down to Miami tomorrow and see what this is all about, hear what they have to say?"

I shook my head. "Dad, I think these so-called scouts are playing you. They tell you what you want to hear to get your money. Don't you watch *20/20*? They're always busting these fake modeling things."

"This is legit," said Dad. "I've checked this agency out. And there are, uh, certain aspects about this modeling offer you should know before you reject the idea."

I smelled something rotten and it wasn't Robby's socks. "Like what?"

"Like you could make a thousand dollars a day," my sister called from upstairs. There was no privacy in this house.

But did she say a thousand? Dollars?

"Actually," Mom said, "we're told the usual rate is fifteen hundred a day. I think she said that's for catalog modeling. Right, Howard?" He nodded. "For magazines it's less. Like a few hundred."

Dad adjusted his glasses and said, "The financial aspect might take care of your tuition."

The financial aspect might take care of my tuition. To Yale. I might still be able to go to Yale.

He continued, "A few months of modeling in Miami could make you enough so that, when it's added to what's left of your college fund, it'll be sufficient to cover the cost."

This was it. My way to get there. My heart started to race with excitement.

But modeling? Me? It was so exploitative, so against everything I stood for.

"But if you don't want to try it, that's okay," Dad said. "We know it's not your thing. And you could get a free ride to a state school, I'm sure. You know, the University of Florida has a pretty good English program. It's not Yale, but . . ." He stopped, seeing the expression on my face. UF wasn't Yale. Nothing else was Yale, and he knew that.

Beautiful was the word they'd used. *Beautiful*. Wow. That was so utterly . . . cool. I looked in the mirror again, trying to see what it was they saw. Maybe it was there and I had some kind of partial blindness or something. "If you decide to do this, our only concern is you living in Miami," Dad said.

Ex-squeeze me?

"Miami? Why would I be living in Miami?"

"There's no modeling out here in Comet. You'd have to move to Miami."

Move to Miami? Wait, what about my life here?

Yeah, what about your life here, Allee? What's so great about it? A crappy job at Wal-Mart with your grandmother, a school full of buttheads, a full academic load, a family who's crowding you, and a sister who now hates you.

Okay, I didn't care if it was modeling or strawberry picking they were offering, any offer to get out of here was looking pretty good.

And any offer that could make me enough money to go to Yale in the fall was worth looking into.

"What do you know about this business?"
the King said to Alice.
"Nothing," said Alice.

chapter ⑤

The lobby of Finesse Model and Talent Management had a red carpet, which was really perfect, because getting past the reception area was like trying to crash the Oscars. The receptionist was totally suspicious of my parents and me, to the point where I was thinking maybe we didn't really have an appointment. She told us to wait, so now we were sitting on black leather couches facing a window, listening to her chirp, "Finesse, please hold," about nine hundred times into her headset and say things like, *"Guten Morgen,* Fritz, I'll get Dimitri. Dimitri, client on five."

I'd brought a book to read, but I was really distracted. Outside, the pink sidewalk on Ocean Drive was full of South Beachers gliding by on Rollerblades, hanging out in cafés, and walking mini-dogs. Two men were strolling down the sidewalk holding hands and laughing, and a woman was zipping by on a scooter wearing nothing but a bikini and a backpack. If I shifted my gaze, I could see roof after roof of pastel-colored art deco hotels. They looked like they were made of candy. Hard to believe Cape Comet was only four hours away. An Alice in Wonderland feeling was coming over me, like this big window was the looking glass, and I was Alice about to step through it, into a different world on the other side.

Twenty minutes passed. Then thirty. It gave me time to check out the framed magazine covers lining the walls. *L'Uomo Vogue, Marie Claire, Petra, Elle, Dietra.* All I could think of was what my sister had said to me last night. That was harsh. And I did *not* think everything was about me. I completely agreed with her that she should be the one sitting here, not me. I wondered if my parents were thinking the same thing. Even my mother looked more like a model than I did in her red sweater dress.

The receptionist hadn't stopped fielding calls. What did she do if she had to go to the bathroom? After forty-five minutes, a Keira Knightley look-alike walked up to us and gave us each a quick handshake. "Hi, sorry about the wait. It gets crazy this time of year." Her British accent could cut glass. Maybe it really was Keira. "You must be Allee." She checked out the sunglasses on top of my head, which had tape on them thanks to Robby stepping on them this morning; my bitten-down nails; and my jeans, which had looked good on me last night in front of my full-length mirror but were, I was noticing now, a little too short. At least I had the dangling faux-pearl earrings The Fluff had given me for my birthday last year.

"Right, then, you're to meet Monique first, then Momma after. Follow me, Allee. Mum, Dad, you too."

"Who's Monique?" my mother asked, getting up.

"Monique Fine," she said in a tone that meant she totally expected us to know who that was. When none of us responded, she added, "The owner? She has to meet potential new faces."

"Momma's not the owner?" my mother asked.

"No. Momma runs TV, film, and commercial print. I'm a booker in her division."

Most of Monique's office was occupied by a desk, crowded with papers, Post-its, photo slides, cards with models' photos on them, and a computer. There was a petite Asian lady sitting behind it with a geometric haircut and short red nails. "Hello, hello, welcome," she said, standing to shake our hands. "I'm Monique Fine. Sit down, sit down." We sat on chairs in front of her desk. Now I could see that she wasn't Asian at all. She was just a victim of Joan Rivers Syndrome. Honestly, plastic surgeons should have an addendum to their Hippocratic oath making them promise they'll never pull a face-lift so tight it stretches people's eyes or gives them Skeletor cheekbones. Talk about do no harm. Yikes.

She carried on about how nice it was to meet us and asked how old I was and what my plans were for the future. Her accent was pure New York. My parents did all the talking while I sat listening to them discuss me as if I wasn't here. After a while she turned to me, winced her collagen-filled lips into something like a smile, and said, "Allee, you have such poe-tential. What we need to do is harness it and let it fly." Wasn't harnessing something the opposite of letting it fly? But I nodded, and she seemed to like that.

"I definitely see what Jay saw in you. Mom, Dad, look at these." She handed my parents some laser prints, and I recognized them as the pictures Jay had taken at the mall. My parents focused on them with the same intensity as Robby searching a page of his *Where's Waldo?* book. "Poe-tential, right? Right?"

These definitely didn't look like my yearbook photos. Waves of hair fanned out around my face. My smile was . . . well, my smile was big. And bright. It was like looking at someone else.

But it was me. It really was me. And I didn't look beige. I looked . . . pretty.

I handed the pictures back to Monique. Her arms were crossed and her eyes were flicking all over my face. "Yeah, the poe-tential is there, but I'm not sure you're right for this business."

"Why not?" Mom asked, her back going straight.

"Well, she's a little stoic, isn't she? Not too smiley."

"But she's smiling in the pictures," Mom said.

"Yes, she photographs well, but I sense a general lack of energy. If her look were more editorial, more fashiony, I wouldn't be concerned. It's bizarre how some girls are as bland as white rice and yet somehow they come alive on film." She leaned forward across her desk and looked me straight in the eye. "But, Allee, your look is commercial, and it's a whole different ballgame. You have to have some personality for clients to book you. You haven't said one word."

"Sorry," I said.

Mom cleared her throat and said, "I assure you she has personality." Afterward, her eyeballs shot me hard laser beams carrying a clear message: *Lighten up, Wednesday Addams.*

"We'll see," said Monique. "But of course, it's up to Momma. My bookers are the best in the business. Here, take a look at our agency book." She took out a black and red yearbook-looking book titled *Finesse Model and Talent Management.* "Touch it, Allee. G'head, open it."

I opened to a page that said "Aisha" at the top. Under her name, there was a close-up of Aisha, biting her lip, with smeared lipstick and streaked mascara running down her cheeks. On the opposite page, Aisha was in an ad for Candie's shoes. It looked like she might be naked, but she was holding a big newspaper in front of her. Above that, there was another photo of her on all fours in a teddy and garter belt. *On all fours!* Disgusting. What if I had to exploit myself like that? Dad made a noise like *"Mmphh."* I *"Mmphh*-ed" him right back so he knew there was no way I would let someone take a picture of me in my underwear.

Monique slammed the book shut, barely missing my hand. "I just wanted you to see the quality of girls we rep here, what an opportunity this is for you. But I don't know. I don't sense that you want all this. Do you? Want all this?"

Her question hung in the air. Of course I didn't. That book was a meat catalog. It depicted unrealistic images of beauty, reduced women to objects. And my sister was right. I definitely didn't know anything about fashion or posing. I could make a fool of myself trying this.

"Allee, do you want to model?" Monique asked again. It was code for a whole set of questions. *Allee, do you want to escape your ant bite of a town? Stop suffocating? Do you want to stop working with Abuela at Wal-Mart?* And most important, the Mac Daddy Numero Uno question: *Do you want to have all the money you need to pay for Yale, more money than you ever thought possible?*

And so I said, "Yeah. I want it more than anything else in the world."

• • •

Every wall in the booking room was hung with Lucite racks full of those model picture cards I'd seen in Monique's office. One wall was women, another was men, and another was children. About a dozen people, mostly women wearing jeans, were sitting around interconnected desks wearing headsets, talking and typing into their computers. It looked like a very casual version of NASA Mission Control. Mom was totally gaping at a pregnant lady in a tube top showing off a stretched-out butterfly tattoo across her belly. Everyone here looked like they were born with the supercool gene. Once again, I was aware of my short, farty jeans. I should have snuck a trendy skirt from The Fluff's closet.

We met with Momma in the conference room. I didn't know what I was expecting, but it wasn't this. Her sixty-something face was a cross between Ozzy Osbourne and a basset hound, jowly but sweet. I couldn't help but relax a little. "Oh, Allee," she said in a manly cigarette voice, "you're just as adorable as Jay said."

Somehow I had to fake that energy Monique was talking about. It was hitting me that this was for real. This model madness could really pay for my dream college. I had to convince Momma I had what it takes. I had to fake it. No more Wednesday Addams for me. *Think, Allee. Personality plus, mojo, cutesy-wootsy, think . . . The Fluff!* "Thank you, I'm like, so happy to finally meet you," I said, my voice bursting with fruit flavor. "We've heard so much about you and I'm like, so excited to be here. Is Momma your real name?" Dad was looking at me like I'd sprouted facial hair. Mom was a different story. Her eyes were glistening with pukey joy.

"No, sweetie, it's Gabriella Diamond, but some actors started calling me Momma Gabby years ago, and then the name just stuck." Momma sat at the head of the table and I sat on one side, my parents on the other. There was a computer, TV, electronic equipment, some cameras and a tripod in the corner. The wall behind me was glass, looking out into the booking room. There were a lot of glass doors and cutouts here, like this place was designed by a voyeur. Model cards and actors' head shots were hanging everywhere.

"You have actors here too, not just models?" I asked.

"Oh, sure," Momma said. "This isn't strictly a model agency, it's a model and *talent* agency, which is one of the reasons we're so sought after. Our TV department is the best in town. We rep all kinds of talent—athletes, actors, you name it. Did you know South Florida is one of the top locations for commercials nationally?"

"Yes," I said. I'd researched the Miami modeling industry on the Internet last night and it said that.

"Now, Allee, let's talk about you," Momma said. "I've seen your pictures. Did you bring any more with you today?"

"I have some," my mother said, whipping out a stack from her purse. I recognized them from the NASA beach picnic.

Momma shuffled through them quickly and went, "Well, you certainly look great in a bathing suit. And the camera loves you. I think you have a look we can use right now. You're dark, but you're not too edgy."

"What's edgy?" I asked.

"An edgy look is one that's editorial, more hard-core. Not like you. Your look is girl next door, and that's very bookable these days. We could use you for the Latin market as well as the Anglo. The important thing is that you have the Latina look, but it's not *too* Latina, which is good. Do you speak Spanish?"

"No."

"I do," Mom said. What, did Mom think they were going to sign her? Her inner Abuela was showing.

"Oh, here's our Greek god," Momma said. "Dimitri books fashion. Dimitri, meet Allee. Isn't she cute?"

Dimitri gave me the up and down eye sweep and said, "Hi, Gorge." He was the one who was gorge. His brown shoulder-length hair had that tousled, just-got-out-of-bed look, but it looked carefully styled that way. My guess was he worked on his five o'clock shadow too. It was too perfect. "Allee, Jay said you're sixteen, yes?"

"Yeah, I skipped first grade, so—"

"You're not right for the high-fashion jobs, but I can still use you on my board. I think you will book the fresher teen editorial jobs, maybe some catalog, some junior work. You could book young adult too, like early twenties. I can already think of some clients I can send your comp to."

"She's only sixteen!" Dad boomed out of nowhere, scaring the crap out of all of us. "She doesn't do anything adult!"

Momma said, "Howard—it is Howard, right? We'll only send her out for whatever castings are appropriate for her age and her look. Allee doesn't have to do anything she's not comfortable with."

"What's a comp?" I asked.

Momma pointed to the model cards on the walls. "Those are composite cards. It's what you take to show clients, like your business card."

A phone buzzed on the table, and the receptionist's voice said, "Dimitri, Odile on three. Says it's an emergency."

What could possibly be an emergency in modeling? He rattled off what could only be Greek cursing, and then he stood up and kissed me on both cheeks! Then he walked out so fast that by the time I said "Bye," he was already gone. My mother craned her neck to catch a glimpse of him before the door closed. Gross. She was old enough to be his mother.

"So how soon can this young lady move down here?" Momma asked my parents. "We have a casting for Roxy clothing next week and she'd be perfect for it. It's mid-January. We're hitting the peak of season now. We can't wait too much longer to try her out. The season starts winding down in late April. By late spring, it's dead around here."

"I can be here as soon as you want," I said in my new perky way.

"Where is the model apartment?" Dad asked, his forehead scrunching up with worry. He and Mom exchanged glances.

"On Euclid, just four blocks from here. Her rent will just get deducted from her earnings. There are models staying there now."

"Allee's never left home, not even for sleepaway camp," my mother said. "Her sister either. We like our kids close to home."

Momma patted her hand, obviously sensing the overprotective vibe. "Trust me, folks, she'll be in good hands. These girls are like my own kids. They don't call me Momma for nothing, you know."

The next parts of their conversation faded in and out. The thought of living with models filled me with panic. They were probably older than me and really sophisticated. Or super-skinny and snobby. Yeah, they were all gonna be beautiful girly-girls with zero IQ who were really into fashion and who wouldn't get me at all.

chapter 6

This was happening really fast. I was feeling the need to do some deep breathing and download all this. I was also feeling the need to pee, so I excused myself and used the ladies' room. After I was done, I walked out and heard a man with a Cuban accent calling, "Yoo-hoo, girlfriend. Excuse me." I kept walking. There was nothing more mortifying than thinking someone was calling you when it was someone else they wanted. Now the voice was right behind me. "Hello, girl with a pearl earring."

I turned around and looked down at a guy wearing a T-shirt that said PLEASE DON'T FEED THE MODELS. He almost bumped into me. All ninety-eight pounds of him. "You dropped this." He handed me my earring. "It just fell off. Ooh, look, there's the back." He plucked the tiny back off the floor and handed it to me.

"Omigod, thank you. Someone gave them to me. She'd kill me if I lost them."

"I know what you mean. I lost my friend's leather pants once and he never spoke to me again."

"How did you lose your pants?"

"Listen, if I had a buck for every time someone asked me that . . ."

I liked this little guy. "I'm Allee," I said, holding out my hand.

"Miguel." He shook my hand with his delicate one. He looked about my age. "I'm a junior booker, Dimitri's assistant, but my real job description is just to keep him calm. That's it, that's my whole job. So was Monique hard on you up there?" I hesitated, not sure what I should say. "I mean was she tough on you? She's been so crabby lately. Issa Lopez left Monique last week and signed with Irene Marie. Monique and Momma are livid. Issa left a hole in the board, but you're exactly her type. Brynn's her type too, but she's cooled off some. You, though, you're going to be hot. Trust me, they need you."

What kind of cryptic *Da Vinci Code* language was this fast-talking Miguel speaking? It wasn't Spanish or English, and I definitely didn't *comprendo*. "Who's Irene Marie?"

"Who's Irene Marie? Who's Irene Marie?" He fake-gasped for air. Then he calmed down. "Okay, here's the dealio. Irene's got an agency a few blocks away. One of our best girls left Monique and went to Irene. And Monique *hates* it when another agency gets our talent. It's a diva vs. diva thing, happens all the time in South Beach." He pronounced it "South Bitch." "But she's very worked up about you, girlfriend. That's why she made Dimitri go meet you. Listen, can you do me a favor?"

"Sure."

"Can you walk on my back?"

"Walk on your what?"

"My back. It'll only take a minute." He dropped to the floor and lay on his stomach. "Go on. Don't be shy. Just take off your shoes." I glanced around. I could see the booking room and they could see me, but nobody was paying any attention. Like this was perfectly normal around here. So I kicked off my flip-flops and stepped on him.

I thought I was going to paralyze him. "Are you sure this isn't hurting you?"

"No, it's good. Now walk. Move your feet." I took baby steps. He was all bones. My weight was going to crush him. "Aaahh, that's it." I looked out into the booking room. One of the bookers was shouting, "You said this was for catalog only! There are billboards all over Costa Rica with her face. You must pay!" The pregnant booker was weighing a woman on a scale. They were talking quietly but I overheard, "They didn't book you because they were afraid you wouldn't fit into the clothes. That should be a red flag to you that you need to lose weight." Another voice, a man this time, called out, "Hey, Tina, they want advertorial. What's the rate for him?"

Crack. Oh no. There goes his spine. I froze, waiting. "*Ay, Dios mio,*" he moaned, letting out a long sigh. "Thank you. You're fantabulous."

Keira hurried past us, bumping into me and stepping over him. "Bloody hell, Miguel, could you possibly do this somewhere else?"

Miguel scrambled to his feet and curved his hands out like claws, hissing like a cat. "Be careful of that Kate," he whispered to me. "She spies on all of us, and she's the worst gossip. And she's *loca*. Actually believes she looks like Keira Knightley, can you believe that?"

"That's crazy."

"Isn't it?"

"Miguel!" Dimitri's voice rang out. "Where the devil are you?"

"Screw him," Miguel whispered. "I'm on break. I'll walk you to the conference room."

When we got there my mother was saying, ". . . were hoping you could show her how to present herself better, you know, use makeup, do her hair."

"Oh, we will. And she'll need to take an on-camera workshop, get some training. Hi, Miguel. Listen, could you show Allee the apartment? I just need to go over some details on the contract with the Rosens. We'll meet you two there."

My parents were looking at the contract already.

Omigod.

The apartment building looked like a birthday cake. It was square and stucco, with a lavender and yellow paint job, wrought-iron balconies, and one of those white fountains next to the entrance, the kind with a little kid peeing. Miguel opened the front door to a small foyer with terra-cotta tiles and a staircase. "You guys are downstairs, number three." He knocked and rang the bell, but there was no answer. "Anybody home?" He turned the doorknob and shoved it open. "No way, they left it open? If Monique finds out, she'll rip them a new one."

We walked in. It smelled like stale cigarette smoke and something else, like lentils or hay. On the left, there was a kitchenette and just past it, an open door, but I couldn't see what was inside from where I was standing. On the right, there was a rectangular living room that must have doubled as a bedroom because I saw bunk beds. Along one wall of the rectangle, there was a turquoise futon, a matching beanbag, and a white coffee table, and along the opposite wall, there was a TV and two bunk beds, one right after the other, like train cars. Behind that, there was a closed door with a full-length mirror attached to it. The far end of the room had a white chest of drawers and a window. The shades were closed, but in the dim light I could see plastic cups, magazines, and an overflowing ashtray on the coffee table. Shoes were scattered all over the floor. Most of the beds looked slept in, with hangers of clothes suspended from the ends of each top bunk.

How was I going to live here? I couldn't think or relax when there was a mess like this. It was like noise to me. Miguel opened the shades. "Most of them are working or out on castings, probably. I know Claudette is out of town. She gets back in a few weeks. You'll have that top bunk, the one that's empty, on top of Summer."

"How many girls live here?" I asked.

"Right now? Five. But sometimes girls stay here for a few days if we have an important casting for them or a job. We always have an extra bed or two."

"Who's there?" a girl's voice called from the room next to the kitchen, the one with the open door. I followed Miguel into it. Sitting on the floor between two more bunk beds were two blond women with porcelain skin and the longest legs I'd ever seen.

One had high, sharp cheekbones and short hair. The other had long, curly hair, a round face, and big Betty Boop eyes. They were folding laundry and watching *SpongeBob SquarePants* on a TV suspended from the ceiling. "Hi, Miguel," they said together. Neither one was wearing a drop of makeup, and they were incredible-looking. They were both so impossibly beautiful, I had to force myself not to stare.

"Hey, you guys. Irina, Vlada, this is Allee. She's new and she'll be moving in soon." They both said hi and went back to their laundry. No "where are you from," no "nice to meet you," nothing. We walked back out to the living room and Miguel said, "They're from one of the stans."

"The stans?"

"You know, Kazakhstan, Ubikkistan, Pakistan, whatev."

"We are from Lithuania, you barnacle head!" one of them shouted. Then I heard them speaking what I guessed was Lithuanian. They sounded pissed.

"They learned English from watching American cartoons," Miguel said, lowering his voice. "Monique thought they'd be a great investment, but she can't get them arrested. Truth. Come here." He took me into the kitchenette. "Now whatever you do, don't turn on the oven." He opened the oven door with a flourish to show me folded T-shirts and shorts stacked on the oven racks. "None of them cook, so they just use this as a chest of drawers. And there's more where that came from." Miguel flipped open the cabinets. All of them were stacked with tanks, sweats, belts, purses, and lots of hair clips and bandannas and things that sparkled.

This place was bursting at the seams with clothes. A lump of fear was forming inside my stomach. I was so apparel-challenged.

I didn't have a fraction of what these girls had. They'd probably laugh at my measly wardrobe. Everything they had looked expensive and designer-ish. My sister dropped designer names constantly, but like most people in Comet, I didn't know a Gucci from a Pucci. Maybe she could help me out and lend me some of her clothes, if she ever spoke to me again.

I opened the fridge. Not much there, just a few Tupperware containers, some coffee creamer, apples, Diet Cokes, bottled water, and two plastic jugs with Kool-Aid-looking drinks. "What's the difference between the green juice and the red juice?"

"About two weeks, probably, knowing these slobs."

A toilet flushed. The door at the end of the living room near the bunk beds opened. Someone wearing sweatpants, a hooded sweatshirt that said NEW JERSEY CHARM SCHOOL, and an eye mask came out. Whoever it was looked like the Unabomber.

Miguel clutched his chest and went, "*Coño*, Brynn, what are you wearing sweats for? This is Miami. It's eighty degrees outside."

Brynn lifted her eye mask up. "I wouldn't have to if the damn Russians didn't keep the AC so friggin' cold it's like Siberia in here. I'm freezing my ass off." She had one of those hoarse, gravelly voices. She yawned and stretched as she walked up to us. "What time is it?"

Miguel was gathering up cups. "Twelve-thirty. Listen, Brynn, get a garbage bag. You guys have to help me clean up. Irina! Vlada! This girl's parents will be here in a few minutes. I think Momma's coming too." He turned to me. "That's the real reason Momma sent us here before your parents. She didn't want you to see all this *mierda* either, but whatev, you were with me."

56

Brynn pulled off her eye mask and flipped her hood down, checking me out. I'd been checked out more times today than I'd ever been checked out in my whole life. Her olive skin and light brown eyes reminded me of my own. "Who the hell are you?" she asked.

"I'm, uh, Allee."

"You both have similar coloring, you know," said Miguel, sweeping up the kitchen. "That's funny. They usually don't like to have too many with the same look on one board. Although maybe it's because you're younger, Allee. You two might not get sent out for the same jobs."

"Might not," Brynn said. "But if we do . . ." She stepped closer to me so we were face-to-face. "Let the games begin."

Whoa.

chapter 7

I went home, packed up, and was flying down I-95 in my Beetle
convertible just two days later. Okay, well, maybe not flying. I was
only going sixty-five. I obeyed the speed limit signs. But it was still
fast enough for my hair to be flapping behind me like a crazy flag
and fast enough so that I couldn't see my parents' SUV following me
in my rearview mirror anymore (they'd insisted on going down, too,
to get me settled in). My top was down, my radio was blasting, and I
was blissed out and feeling free as I headed back to South Beach.

Even my car was feeling the excitement. Seriously. Have you
ever really looked at a Volkswagen Beetle? They have faces. I'd
have sworn my car was smiling. I wasn't too sure what it was smiling about, though, since the red paint was scratched in places and

there was a rip in the black upholstery. It was really a used piece of junk, if you want to know the truth. But it was cool, all mine, and it got me out of Comet, so I'd always love it for that.

I did have some fears fluttering around in my belly, though. Brynn had freaked me out. She scared me. But the instant she said *Let the games begin*, I was ready to play against her. I don't know if it was the intense way she got up in my face and challenged me or what, but something came over me, an I'll show her feeling. I'd always been competitive about stuff I cared about, like grades or cross-country, but this was different. I didn't know anything about being in front of the camera. But I suddenly wanted to jump into the modeling ring, wanted to prove myself, even if it meant butting heads with an intimidating chick like Brynn.

And who didn't want to be told they're pretty enough to be a model? Let's be real. The scouts and the bookers were excited about me, and I was flattered. Back home, I believed strong, smart women shouldn't be valued by their appearance. But all the attention I was getting in South Beach was like a feel-good drug. I was totally disoriented. Maybe everybody's dirty little secret was that they wanted to be beautiful.

It sure turned out to be mine.

"If you miss a casting, you better have a damn good reason. And if it happens again, I drop you. Miss a casting for a national commercial, you don't get a second chance. Same goes if you don't show for a booking. You're gone." Momma and I were in the conference room at the big table. I was taking notes. Her growly man-voice was clipped and sharp, all business. "You might have six or seven castings in one day, all within ten blocks, right here

on the strip. Or you might have none for your type. It's an un-
predictable business. TV castings are all over the city, and we like
it when models go together. Don't be late to a casting, and don't
ever, ever be late to a booking. Ever. All you have to do is show up
on time with your voucher for them to sign so you can get paid,
and don't forget to have a good attitude. And by the way, 'on time'
means ten minutes early in this business. If you're not sure where
a location is, go there in advance and do a practice run." She
handed me a paper. "Here's a list of on-camera workshops we rec-
ommend. Try to take the ones given by casting directors. They're
the best, and they'll keep you in mind for commercials if you take
their workshop. Lori Wyman's is really good. Any questions?"

Yeah, how about, could you repeat all that? "No."

Her basset hound/Ozzy face crinkled into a grin. She patted my
hand. "You're going to do just fine, sweetie. Don't look so nervous."

"I'm not." Yeah, right. I'd been a bundle of nerves ever since I
got here a couple of hours ago. My parents just left and I was trying to let go of this gnawing ache they left in me. I didn't expect to
feel this way. I thought I'd feel independent, happy to start enjoying my new freedom, and instead I was fighting back tears. They'd
taken me to lunch and made a big production out of saying good-
bye. Mom got all teary-eyed and made me promise to call and eat
right and take my vitamins. Dad told me to come home and visit
soon, and then he gave me an envelope with five hundred dollars
inside. So even though I was experiencing some pangs from cutting the parental strings, I was also feeling kinda rich.

Momma coughed and chugged her water bottle. "Good. I can
start sending you out as soon as your comp is done. Your comp is
the first step, then we'll put together your portfolio book. Miami's

a great market to build up your book. We can set you up with a testing photographer to get you started. Now. Let's talk communication. I told your mom to get you a BlackBerry or a Sidekick." I pointed to the BlackBerry clipped onto my jeans. "Good. We'll e-mail your details most of the time, but stop by or call and check in every couple of days, okay? Swing by Dimitri's table too."

"Okay."

"Oh, and here." She slid something across her desk. It was a date book, black with red letters that spelled out *Finesse*. "Write your castings and bookings in this agenda and always have it with you. I know, I know, you have your BlackBerry, but you kids lose them, delete things, and I don't know what. I like to have a backup, so just write everything down. Kapeesh?"

"I will."

"You bet your ass you will, sweetie."

The phone buzzed and the receptionist's voice announced, "Sorry to interrupt, but Kate's going crazy back there. Two more castings came in and she is *fuh-reaking*."

"All right, help's on the way. Come on, Allee, you might as well see my hideout. We'll finish this meeting later."

She took me across the booking room and behind the staircase to a boxy little room with two cluttered desks, some chairs and filing cabinets, a fax machine, and stained carpeting. "Welcome to the TV department." She sat down at one of the desks, waving me into a chair. "Monique hides us back here like a bastard child."

The walls were wallpapered with actors' head shots. There were people of all ages and ethnicities, and some most definitely didn't look like models. Momma noticed me looking. "My division books movies, videos, commercials, you name it."

The Keira Knightley clone was typing and talking into her headset. "Heidi, Kate. Got a national for a Lexus spot. I need a yummy mummy twenty-eight to thirty-two years old. No carpool types. They want a MILF. It's right up your alley. Call me, love." She turned to Momma. "I'm going mad."

"Time slots?"

"Only four."

"Did you call Sandy?"

"Nah. She's jumped the shark lately. Ever since she cut her hair."

"What else?"

"Progresso beans. Latina Mom and high school daughter, no dialogue. Nonunion for Mexico. Three days, fifteen hundred a day, buyout."

"What about Allee here?" Momma said.

"Brilliant. Welcome aboard, Allee."

The phone rang. Momma picked it up. "Claudette. Casting tomorrow. I need you to be a teen prostitute for a new crime show pilot, mmm-kay?"

Another line rang. Kate pushed a button on her phone and said into her headset, "Hey, Michael, can you belch on request?"

"No, not a Pretty Woman type," Momma said into the phone. "Think Biscayne Boulevard crackhead, dirty hair, clumpy mascara, white spandex."

"Can you belch the alphabet?" Kate asked into her headset. "It's for Alpha-Bits cereal. The script says, uh, let's see here, 'Alpha-Bits is so fun to eat, it turns grown-ups into kids.'"

"Just one line," said Momma. "You have to say, 'Hey, Daddy.' Say it real sexy. Right. Just like that."

"Right, the whole alphabet," said Kate. "You can? Brilliant. Let's hear it."

Somebody's phone buzzed and the receptionist's voice called out, "Brynn's on line two again." Brynn. There goes my heart, going into manic, kerblanging rhythm. It was as if she was in the room. "Should I put her through?" the receptionist asked. "She wants to know why you won't submit her for that L'Oréal casting coming up."

Momma pounded her desk. "Dammit, I told her a thousand times. She's not right for it. Her hair isn't thick enough and it's too dry. I can't talk to her right now. Get rid of her."

My hair was thick and shiny. The scouts loved my hair. Jay went on and on about it at the mall. Excuse me, great hair right in front of you, ladies. *What about me for that L'Oréal thing?* I pulled my hair out of its ponytail, shook it, played with it. *Come on, Momma, eyes on me, stop looking at your computer screen.*

Kate noticed me. "Hey, Momma, what about Allee for L'Oréal?" she asked.

Momma's jowls spread into a smile. "As a matter of fact, Miss Allee, you'd be great for it."

Nobody was home in the apartment. It was neater than the last time I'd seen it. It actually looked cute. Before, I hadn't noticed the pretty aqua-colored carpeting that matched the futon, or the paintings of Mediterranean islands everywhere.

Miguel came over to deliver some cleaning supplies and stayed for a while. He went through my suitcase with me and pulled out a few things he thought would be good for castings. There wasn't much he liked. "Your biggest problem," he said, "is color." He held up a gray tank and wrinkled his nose. "If a fart could be seen, it would be this color. *Blech.*" Then he flung it across the room, adding, "It doesn't do you justice. Your hair, your skin, your whole *you* is too fabulous for gray. You need jewel tones, Allee girl. I'm talking ruby, emerald, topaz."

After hanging out and making himself a cup of coffee, he'd had to leave for some dinner meeting with Dimitri, so now I was alone. Okay, back to my notes. I wrote down everything Momma had said: *Keep nails short and clean. No brightly colored nail polish. Don't get too tan. Little color okay, no tan lines. Go easy on jewelry and makeup for print go-sees. Want to look like blank canvas, healthy, fresh. Image is light, fun. Think happy virgin.*

Must wax eyebrows and do Brazilian down below!!!!!! Take two Aleve fifteen minutes before appointment. Be careful when smiling not to show too much gum. Practice smiling with tongue pressed behind teeth to hide any black space. Hair is fab, don't change a thing, want to run naked through it. (????) Buy slinky dresses, body-hugging clothes—try Urban Outfitters, Sixth and Collins. Wear bright colors, def show midriff. Don't wear black tops for TV castings, will look like floating head on tape.

This beanbag wasn't that comfortable. Or maybe it was just me who wasn't comfortable. If only the knot in my stomach would go away. I was waiting for something to happen, but I didn't know what. Forget about that rich-and-independent sensation I'd had earlier. I was the new kid on the first day of school and I was feeling lost. I kept thinking about my sister. She was probably dying to know what had happened to me on my first day in the modeling biz, but she was so stubborn, no way would she pick up the phone first.

I started to dial home, but hung up quickly when I heard a key turning in the lock.

It was Brynn. Her face was professionally made up, smoky eyes, red lipstick. She was wearing that NEW JERSEY CHARM SCHOOL sweatshirt again, with black leather pants and pointy boots. "Well, well, well, if it isn't my competition. What's your name again?"

"Allee."

She stretched out on the futon, put her feet on the coffee table and her hands behind her head. My beanbag was next to the futon. She looked down at me on the beanbag and I looked up at her on the futon.

Seconds ticked by. This was stupid. Someone had to say something. I tried to start a little conversation going with, "I like your makeup."

"Thanks."

Why did I compliment her? Why, why, why? "Where are you from?" I asked. She smirked and pointed to her sweatshirt. "New Jersey? Oh." Long, awkward silence. "I'm from Cape Comet. It's here. In Florida."

"Never heard of it." She lit up a cigarette, blew smoke in my direction. Thanks for asking if I minded. Which I did.

"Um, I didn't unpack yet. Do you know where I can put my stuff?"

"Well, let's see. We all share the closets, but they're pretty full right now. The top three drawers of the dresser are mine. Bottom three are Summer's. Claudette uses the kitchen. Vodka and Tonic had stacked milk crates, but they took them when they left. Wish I could help you."

Yeah, I bet. "Who are Vodka and Tonic?"

"The Russians. You met them."

"Where did they go?"

She shrugged. "I heard they're waitressing somewhere. Monique gave 'em the boot. They were deadweight. Couldn't book any jobs." Irina and Vlada got the boot? They of the long legs and porcelain skin and stunning beauty, the most perfect-looking humans I'd ever seen, got the boot? If *they* got the boot, what chance did I have?

Brynn tossed her head toward the bedroom next to the kitchen. "I got their room." She pointed her cigarette at the bunk beds across from us. "You're sleeping out here."

She smoked. I sat. I decided to try a conversation one more time. "Were you on a casting today?"

"No. I had a booking, actually." Her eyes narrowed. "Were you?"

"What?"

"On a casting."

"Oh, no. I don't even have a comp card yet."

"So you've never modeled before?"

"Uh-uh."

"You've never done anything?"

"No."

She looked satisfied. She was obviously really experienced. "Do you always wear your BlackBerry clipped to you like that?"

"Why?"

She shrugged, blew a smoke ring. "It's just very Revenge of the Nerds, that's all." I felt my mouth open a little, beyond my control. I didn't know how to respond to someone like this. "Sorry, I don't filter well. You'll have to get used to it, Allee."

And then it occurred to me how to respond. "I didn't have any castings today, but Momma said she's going to send me to the L'Oréal casting coming up." Now it was her jaw that dropped. I'd caught her off guard. It gave me a charge, made me feel stronger. "My comp should be ready by then. Momma says I'm perfect for it." Ha! Maybe I was finally getting more assertive. "So I guess I might get some of the castings you don't. You'll have to get used to it, Brynn." I ruled!

She raised an eyebrow. "How old are you?"

"Almost seventeen."

For some insane reason, she was smiling. "You talk a pretty good talk for almost seventeen. I'm nineteen, in case you're wondering." She put out her cigarette in the ashtray. "Just be careful. This market is pretty cutthroat, you know. It's competitive out there." She yawned and gently pulled off one row of false eyelashes. "Take me, for instance. I'm not about to let some girl who looks like me walk in here out of Cape Hicksville or wherever the hell you're from, and take what's mine. Mine, as in, my castings, my clients, my bookings, you hear what I'm saying?" Now she was pulling off the false eyelashes from her other eye. "That's just not going to happen. Believe me. I'll do whatever it takes to make sure it doesn't happen."

Omigod. Was that a death threat?

The front door opened, and a model I hadn't seen before came in. "Hey, y'all," she said, smiling. "You must be Allee." She was in a bikini and a mesh cover-up that covered nothing. Her body was a perfect ten, athletic and curvy at the same time, like a *Sports Illustrated* swimsuit model. Maybe she *was* a *Sports Illustrated* model.

"Hey, Summer," Brynn said. Summer. That's exactly what she looked like. She had yellow hair, thick, with white-blond highlights, wide-set blue eyes, full lips, and a sprinkling of pale freckles. Like with Irina and Vlada, it was hard not to stare, but there was more than beauty to this girl. I couldn't say why, but it was like some mysterious force was pulling my eyes to her, as if she was plugged into a secret light source the rest of us didn't have.

The phone rang. Brynn answered it, "Hi, Ma," like she was expecting the call. She went into Irina and Vlada's old room, shutting the door behind her. Wow. It was weird to think of Brynn having a mother. Her mom probably wore leather jackets and carried a switchblade.

"'Scuse the way I'm dressed," Summer said. "I just came from a casting."

"For bathing suits?" I asked.

"Nope, for a Ludacris video."

We were quiet for a few seconds, listening to the muffled sounds of Brynn talking on the phone in the next room, followed by her shouting, "Ma, what the hell's the matter with you? You can't eat ice cream every night. You got high cholesterol."

"Miguel says you're from Florida," Summer said. She pronounced Miguel *Mee-gayal*. "Zat right?"

"Yeah. I've never been away from home before," I found myself telling her. I was totally mesmerized by her smile, her warmth, her everything.

"Me either. I'm a Georgia girl myself. It's hard at first, but you'll get used to it. How old are you?"

"Sixteen. I'll be seventeen next month."

"I'm eighteen."

"Ma, I don't want to hear it!" Brynn belted out from behind the door. "Shut your pie hole and get on a treadmill already, or stop complaining you're fat."

"Well, I know how scary it is to be away from home for the first time," Summer said. "I'll show you the ropes."

"Thanks."

"Where's your stuff? I'll help you unpack. I got some drawer space you can use. It ain't much, but . . ."

"Thanks," I said again.

She had the energy Monique was talking about. She was bubbly and sweet and cheerful and all the things I wasn't. If we were back in Comet I'd have hated her on sight, or at the very least, lumped her in with Hillary High Beams and her crew, or been intimidated by her. I'd definitely keep my distance.

But Summer's smile looked real. "If there's anything you need, any questions, jest give me a holler, 'kay? When I came here I didn't know nothin'."

I wanted to hate her, but I couldn't. She was just nice. It was that simple. Okay, so maybe I wouldn't be having intellectual discussions with her, like on the use of double negatives, for example, but I could live with this girl. She was a relief after Brynn. At least she was kind, and kindness was always a good thing to have around.

From the other room, I heard, "Ma, you shoulda seen that new girl just now when I told her she better watch it. She almost crapped her pants!"

Especially when you thought you were going to need it.

chapter 8

We were on a five-minute break, and thank God for the blanket. Underneath it, all I had on was a wet, flowered bikini and tiny cover-up shorts. It turned out the beach was freezing at seven a.m. Well, freezing by Miami-in-January standards. It was about fifty-five degrees. "Can't have a comp card without a bathing suit shot," Momma said when I asked why I had to pose in a bikini for my first test shoot. Not that I had anything to hide. I'd been a runner since middle school, so my butt and legs were pretty tight. But just on principle, why did my very first set of pictures have to be all about T and A?

Momma also told me I'd love the photographer. She was right. Sean was thirtysomething, bearded, and overtanned, and

I liked the quiet way he was giving me directions. He was also probably the first straight man I'd met in the three days I'd been here. The handful of men in the booking room were all gay, but it was a wide range of gay, from totally obvious to not at all obvious. Miguel registered a ten on the gay-o-meter, and gorgeous Dimitri a one or zero. Dimitri seemed so straight, the way he talked to me and how he kissed me hello, but Miguel assured me he was "gayer than Christmas." Anyway, I knew Sean was straight because a) he kept grabbing the stylist's butt, which was okay because I was pretty sure she was his girlfriend, and b) I saw a *Stuff* magazine in his van, and c) he was listening to Black Sabbath, which I highly doubt was a musical fave among the gay crowd here.

Momma told me this was a very major test with a full crew, that most new faces had a more simple test with just a photographer and an assistant, and some even skipped a test altogether and went to castings with just a Polaroid. She said the agency had a lot of faith in me and wanted to send me out with the best card possible. It was getting me nervous. I mean, they seemed to think I was going to be some great model. What if that didn't happen?

Yesterday we went to three different locations before the rain cut our shooting schedule short. The first was of me sitting on a vinyl-cushioned stool in front of an outdoor window at Cafeteria Café Cubano, sipping a teensy cup of Cuban coffee. Lily, the stylist, put me in a real cuchifrito outfit: red flared minidress, gold heels, flower in my hair, hoop earrings, plastic bangles. Talk about a *hispana mamá* stereotype. The shoot was going great until I felt those damned bugs in the flower. My scalp was all bumpy where they stung me.

For the second shot, I had to walk in front of a parked school bus and pretend I was talking on a cell phone. Every few steps I looked up and said "cheeesebuuurger" real slow into the phone, then walked back and did it again, over and over. This time Lily let me wear my own clothes: favorite Levi's, green polo shirt, Yale backpack. I guessed this look was supposed to be Anglo Allee as opposed to Latina Allee.

The last location was the pink sidewalk right in front of my apartment. I had to ride a bicycle barefoot in a skirt and tank top while smiling and holding up a soda with one hand. Excuse me. Who would do this in real life? The biggest challenge was not crashing the bike into any of the cars that are always parked bumper to bumper along the curb, and also not letting the wind blow my skirt up too much because by accident I put my thong on sideways yesterday, so the shoot could have easily gotten embarrassing if I wasn't careful.

The whole thing got easier when Sean let me sit on the bike and blow giant bubble-gum bubbles. I was actually getting into it until Brynn opened the window and hung her head out, watching. Just my luck, she was home. It threw me off and I couldn't blow any more big ones after that, especially because she was shouting things like "Come on, Allee, you can do better. Sean, tell her she blows." For a pro, Brynn seemed pretty unprofessional.

Today she was nowhere in sight, so I was feeling pretty good. "The light at this hour is amazing," Sean said, adjusting his ponytail and fiddling with his camera. "I've shot all over the world, but I tell ya, the color of the light in Miami is the most beautiful."

"One more round, boss?" asked Sean's assistant. He was Jamaican, and his dreadlocks were tucked under one of those striped knit hats that look like a Jiffy Pop microwave-popcorn bag.

"Yeah," Sean answered, still fiddling with his camera. "Check the exposure again, will you? And hold the reflector facing the water this time. Allee, go stand over there." I took off the blanket and stood in front of the round silver disk that Jiffy Pop was holding up. He held a light meter to my face as Juan, the hair and makeup guy, touched me up with some powder, lip gloss, and blush. Earlier, Juan had done my hair in two Dorothy braids, and Lily had put a canvas hat on me in the same flowered fabric as the bikini top. Okay, so this bathing suit was more cutie-pie than T and A.

Sean squatted down a few yards away from me, pointing the camera upward. "Okay, Allee, take a few steps into the water, get your feet wet. Now act excited. Kick up some water—that's it. Don't look at the camera. These are lifestyle shots, they're supposed to look candid."

There was a stray hair in my mouth. I blew it out and attempted to keep my smile going. Oh, wait. I forgot to kick the water. What did I do with my arms?

"Come on, a bit more energy. Get excited, pretty girl." I was trying, but my movements were awkward and jerky. Sean wasn't clicking away like he did yesterday. I must have looked as stupid as I felt. "You're giving me too much chin. Keep your chin down." He stood up. "This isn't working," he said quietly.

A few yards off, two pudgy old ladies were sitting in aluminum chairs, watching. Their sun-damaged skin was the color and texture of beef jerky. I just knew they were laughing at me. I bet everyone in that yoga class way down the beach was thinking it was too bad I didn't have any natural grace like they did. I wanted to cry. How could I fail at something as simple as taking a stupid picture?

Sean and Lily were whispering. Juan came over to me. "Close your eyes," he said, brushing eye shadow on my lids. "You're too stiff. You need to get loose."

"I know. But I don't know how."

"It's easy. Just be a beautiful girl."

"What do you mean?"

"Until you believe you're beautiful, you're not going to be comfortable with your body. Believe you're beautiful. Open your eyes. Look up." He smeared something under each eye. "So imagine yourself as the girl with the perfect face, the perfect body, a perfect ten. Really see it in your mind." He held up my chin and looked at my face, tapped the top of my head. "It's all up here. Tell yourself you're beautiful, say it in your mind while he's shooting, okay?" I nodded back at him. "Be that girl in your head."

"Okay, let's try something different," said Sean. "Allee, you're getting wet."

Of course I was getting wet. I was standing in the water, you—Hey, why was Lily holding a big plastic pail? Oh no. No. No. She was *not* throwing a bucket of water at me, she was not—

She was. I screamed, jumping out of the way to block the spray. My rear end got soaked anyway, and I heard laughter and orders to jump again. So I did, just as another pail of cold water blasted my legs. I laughed along with the others to show I was Playful, Amusing Allee now, but this was so not even remotely funny or amusing. It totally sucked to be doused in freezing water. But I forced out a laugh, because that's what they wanted.

"Twirl," Sean said. "Now throw your hat up. Great." Great? This was not great. *Whoosh.* Another wave of water, this time courtesy of the ocean. I screamed.

"Scream 'whee,'" said Sean.

"Wh-what?" I asked. My teeth were chattering.

"Scream again, but scream the word 'whee.'" What was he talking about? "Can you do that?"

"Sure. No problem."

"On three. Lily, get ready with the water. Allee, scream 'whee' when the water hits you. One, two . . ." *Wham.* Lily didn't wait for three.

"Wh-whee."

"Louder!" Sean shouted.

"Whee!"

"Louder!"

"WHEEEEEEE!!!" I shrieked with insanity, throwing my arms up and kicking the crap out of the water.

"Got my shot," said Sean, giving me a thumbs-up. I knew where he could put that thumb. I wasn't loving him so much anymore.

But wait. I wasn't stiff. My arms and legs felt connected to my body. My blue lips were smiling for real now. And Sean was clicking like crazy. I arched my back and twirled around in the surf. I was being that girl, like Juan said. *You're beautiful, Allee Rosen. You're a perfect ten. And you can do this.*

But it couldn't be that simple. Just to tell yourself you were beautiful and *poof*, you were.

Could it?

chapter 9

It was Modeltopia. There must have been a hundred girls at this catalog casting, and they were all winners of the genetic lottery: tall, thin bodies, graceful necks, arched eyebrows.

What was I doing here?

This client was more glam than me, and definitely more interesting to look at, starting with his hair. Think Crayola red, like Elmo. Spiky clumps of it, all over his head. Then there were the black, square glasses, unbuttoned leopard-print shirt over a tank, flour-white skin, and red, penciled-in eyebrows, and don't forget the German Arnold Schwarzenegger accent. "We haven't seen you in South Beach before."

"I just got here three weeks ago." Three weeks of castings

every day and not one booking yet. Not even close. This demeaning process might have been worth it if I was making money. I'd gone out for that L'Oréal commercial, made it to the callback, and got the agency all excited, and then they didn't book me. And what a waste of time the Progresso beans casting was. After waiting an hour for the casting director to group me with a Latina "mom," we had to sit at a table and pretend we were eating rice and beans and really enjoying it. Then when the casting director said "Now," we had to suddenly explode with laughter for no reason. From what I knew about beans, they made you explode a different way. And I'd like to know what was in the beans that supposedly made people laugh their heads off, and if it was legal, why didn't they put it in Oreos or something more fun to eat?

"Your book, please," Elmo-hair ordered. I slid my portfolio across the table to him. Mine was nothing like the thick books most of the other models had, full of tear sheets ripped from magazines with all the ads and editorials they'd done. He zipped through my five shots, the ones from my test shoot, and five from another two tests I did, and said: "So you have no experience whatsoever."

"No, I'm a new face." It's the phrase Momma told me to use. "I'm in development." That was another one. Like I was going through a second puberty.

"Ya, we can tell by your book. There's nothing here." He fanned himself with my composite card, the version with ALLEE ROSE printed on the front. Momma liked the image of a rose, thought it would sell me better. The agency had printed two sets of comps, fifty with ALLEE ROSE for Anglo jobs and fifty with ALLEE

77

ROSA for Latin castings, and posted them on their Web site too. Clients could log on with a password and see our comps and portfolios online. Summer's comp said SUMMER J. but I knew neither the "Summer" nor the "J" was real, because the mailing labels on her magazines were addressed to Darlene Mole.

Elmo-hair jabbered something in German to the man sitting next to him, a stumpy dude sporting an unlit cigarette behind his ear, a small hoop earring, and a black bandanna around his head. Pirate Man was looking at me like he had X-ray vision, and it was creeping me out. I guessed he was the photographer. They were usually the straight ones.

Based on all the *"ya, ya"*-ing between the two of them and the way they kept scanning me from top to bottom, it was obvious they were discussing my body. I forced a smile, suppressing my urge to stand on a table and yell "Fresh meat! Come get your fresh meat here!"

There was a girl walking toward me. "Damn, we might as well go home now that April's here," some model whispered behind me.

"Yeah. She books everything," someone else said.

What were they talking about? This April chick had limp hair the color of dead grass and matching freckles carpeting her face like a stain. And she wasn't just skinny, she was bony. The girl looked like she was barely holding on to life, let alone a modeling career.

She was right next to me now and it looked like she was going to say something to me, but no, she stepped right in front of me and what the—? The back of her head was in my face! Where did she get off cutting the line like that? I tapped her bony shoulder blade. She ignored me because Elmo-hair and Pirate Man were popping up from behind the table as if their underwear were on fire. They kissed her on both cheeks, falling all over her. "Ooh, look who's here, April, you're looking fabulous, can't believe we haven't seen you since Eleuthera," and on and on. Now she was talking about some shoot she'd just done, and they were laughing at every stupid thing she said.

What was I, invisible? There was an order here, and number 126, my number, was up. April the Great could take a number like the rest of us. I tapped again. She just gave me her profile, like she couldn't be bothered to turn all the way around. "This'll only take a minute," she said. "I just stopped by to say hi. I'm already booked for this job." Her voice was bland and kinda whiny, as if the prospect of yet another modeling gig was just *muy* inconvenient, like a dental appointment.

"Well, are you done saying hi yet? Because we're in the middle of a casting here." Being assertive was easy when I didn't know the person. This time April turned all the way around to face me. I gestured at the goddesses sitting along the wall behind me. "There's a line, you know." Some nodded, agreeing with me, and one girl even raised her fist to show solidarity. I raised mine too, right back at ya, girlfriend. Except . . . she was listening to her iPod, bobbing her head to the music and not even paying attention to me. She probably just meant "rock on." Oh well, it worked anyway. April kissed the clients *auf Wiedersehen*, stopped to give me a nasty look, and dripped away on her long, toothpick legs.

"So, Allee," said the pirate. "How old are you?"

"Sixteen. Almost seventeen."

79

He clasped his hands behind his head, and a powerful B.O. cloud floated directly into my nostrils. *Ew*. Summer had warned me that afternoon go-sees were thick with the smell of photographers and stylists who'd been shooting on the beach all morning and hadn't showered yet.

"It's so hot in here," Elmo-hair said, taking off his leopard-print shirt. He was wearing a Blink-182 tank underneath. So he was into punk. I wonder if he listened to—

Shprink! (That was the sound of a lightbulb going off in my brain.)

Just as Elmo-hair handed me my book, about to shake my hand and point me toward the exit I'm sure, I took him by surprise. "Do you know Brainless Wankers?"

"No, but give them my number. I'm not picky." He let out a shriek that morphed into giggles. I loved it. Then he stopped abruptly, looking at me with new eyes. "Just a joke, of course. You listen to them?"

I clicked a few keys on my BlackBerry and my ring tone screamed out the Wankers hit song "Beach Life Is Tough." His smile was as big as mine. "I saw them play at Friedens-fest last summer." He turned to Pirate Man and said something that sounded like he was working up a loogie, something like: "*Ichachchchachchchgutenfur* junior line?"

And then Pirate Man went something like: "*Yamitein*Polaroid-*badeanzug.*"

"Allee, we'd like to see you in a bathing suit, please." He pointed behind the elevator. "Go down this hall. We taped a paper sign on the door—Scarlett Print Productions. We take a Polaroid, ya?"

Ya! With a side order of hallelu-*ya!* Maybe I'd finally get booked. Thank you, Brainless Wankers!

Except where was Scarlett Print Productions? There was no sign on any door. I walked into a guys' casting by accident. They all had the best hair I'd ever seen on guys—buzzed short, surfer long and messy, neat and preppy, gelled, blown, highlighted. I recognized a few of them from the agency and we waved to each other. Summer had told me not to go out with any models. She said they were all players. I left and kept looking for Scarlett Print Productions.

Yesterday I'd learned the hard way that sometimes hotels had several castings going on at the same time. Brynn had told me to go to the pool area instead of the conference room, and I wound up showing my book to the wrong client. Turned out he was casting for Marlboro, and you had to be twenty-five to pose for cigarettes, so the client called the agency and yelled at Dimitri for wasting his time. And then Dimitri yelled at me in Greco-English, which, believe me, was a little scary.

I finally found the right room. It was an office with a desk, a floor-length mirror, a hanging rack of clothing, and a bulletin board with composites and Polaroids all over it. A handful of models in bathing suits, including Summer and Brynn, were in the corner. They were watching a lady snap Polaroids of a girl in a bra and underwear. I watched from the doorway until the lady took the girl's comp, stapled it to the Polaroid picture she'd just taken, and said "Next" while another girl walked up to the bare wall to be Polaroided.

Summer waved me over. Brynn didn't even bother to look up, as usual. "Hey, you guys," I said, dropping my big canvas bag, then pulling off my shorts and tank for the fifth time today. My bathing suit was underneath, a dark yellow two-piece.

Summer's face was scrunched in pain from the deep squat she was doing. In a string bikini. I had to ask, "Why are you doing that?"

"Makes your leg muscles pop," she grunted. "Look at the clothes." I tried, but it was hard to see them. Some of the outfits were covered in plastic with composite cards taped to them. One of them was April's. "Shorts and camis. It's a summer line. They're lookin' for fit."

"Oh." Brynn leaned against the wall and watched me join Summer in a halfhearted knee bend. Half of my bathing suit bottom embedded itself where the sun don't shine. How come Summer's didn't do that? "I got lost. There was no sign on the door."

"Yeah," Summer said. "Someone playin' dirty musta ripped it off. Narrows down the competition if people can't find the room. Stuff like that happens sometimes."

"Only in Miami," one of the other models said. "The girls here are like snakes."

"Yeah," her friend agreed. "It's worse here than in New York."

"Nah, New York's just as bad."

I shot a pointed look at Brynn, remembering how she'd directed me to the wrong client yesterday. She glared at me. "What? Are you saying I ripped off the stupid sign?"

"I didn't say anything."

"You gave me a look."

"No, I didn't."

"Yeah, you did and don't lie. Look at me. I don't *need* to play those reindeer games."

82

"Neither do I." Excellent response, Allee. Witty.

"Next," the Polaroid lady called out, saving me.

While Brynn got her picture taken, Summer quietly gave me tips. She'd really taken me under her wing these last few weeks. I didn't know how I'd learn all this stuff without her. "Make sure you smile a whole lot, and don't pose all sexy-like. This here's catalog, not a fashion thing. Here, take my lotion for your legs."

"How do you get your, uh, top to look like that?" I pointed to her perfectly pushed-up, smushed-together breasts.

"What, these?" She cupped herself.

"Yeah. They look so . . . up and out. What's your secret?"

"No secret. Chicken cutlets."

"Really? Chicken cutlets?"

"Yep. Everybody in the business does it. You'd be surprised at how good they work."

"Wow. Who knew? I'll have to pick up KFC for lunch tomorrow."

Summer laughed, throwing her head back. The other models stopped talking to watch her. It was as if her laugh was a performance and she expected everyone to applaud when she was done. "Allee, look." She pulled out a flesh-colored silicone insert from the side of her bathing suit top. It looked like a breast. A chicken breast, to be exact.

Oh.

"Never you mind, Allee. You might be slow, but you'll catch on, you will." Imagine *her* thinking *I'm* stupid! Summer tossed her chin toward Brynn. "Watch how she poses for bathing suit shots. She does it good." Brynn had one leg in front of the other, her front foot angled at two o'clock, front knee slightly bent. It was a more relaxed version of a beauty pageant pose. The lady took four shots of her—front, back, and two profiles. Brynn used that stance every time she turned. "See?" Summer said, demonstrating it for me. "It makes the line of your body look thinner and taller. You should always stand like that for Polaroids, Allee, 'specially since you're not so tall as most of us."

I tried it in front of the mirror. "Good," Summer said. "Bend that knee more and air up your lungs real good." She took a deep breath. I mimicked her. "There ya go, now your chest is bigger so your waist looks smaller. Yep, makes ya look taller, too. It's one of them topical illusions."

"You mean optical."

"What's that?"

"Optical illusions. Not topical."

"Whatever." Whenever Summer got it wrong, she just went "Whatever" and forgot about it. What a stress-free way to go through life. Sometimes I wished I was simpler, like her. She was happier than most people.

"Next," the lady said.

"You go ahead of me," said Summer. "I have to pee real quick."

She took off and I pulled out my composite, handed it to the lady, and walked up to the wall while Brynn slipped on her slinky tube dress and huge sunglasses. "Hey, Allee," she said, strutting toward the door. "Here's a tip from me to you. When you wear a school-bus-yellow bikini?" She stopped, lifted her sunglasses, zeroed in on my backside. "It makes your ass look like a school bus."

Oh no, she was not. She was not going to do that to me. I

knew I didn't have a big butt. It stuck out, yes, like a butt is *supposed* to stick out. And it wasn't as if mine was extra large, like it was the Big Gulp Family Size serving of butts or something. I was a runner. I had well-developed glutes, that's all.

I did not, absolutely *did not* have a big butt.

chapter 10

"Do I have a big butt?"

"For the last time, no."

We were leaving the lobby, weaving through the models still waiting around. I was tagging along behind Summer. "Seriously?"

"Seriously. And stop squeezing your own bee-hind. The clients can see you."

As if Elmo-hair and Pirate Man were wasting their eyes on me. Summer was the one every eye was on, with her long, buttery princess-in-the-castle hair and that electric glow she had. I felt the stares. When I went somewhere with her it was like being next to a chandelier. She was oblivious to the heads swiveling or, sometimes, the whispers. Those reactions were such a part of her environment that she didn't really see them anymore, like the palm trees at every corner.

My feet were killing me. Today I'd walked to five castings, all over the art deco district. That spot on the front steps of the hotel looked like a good place to rest. I sat down, right near a gaggle of models smoking. Summer stretched out next to me. "Tell ya what, Allee, you need to git some Rollerblades or a bike, maybe a scooter. Why didn't you drive your cute little car?"

"There's no parking here. Ever. I shouldn't have bothered bringing my car down."

"You'll need it for the commercial castings. Casting directors ain't all on the beach." She lifted a pair of Rollerblades out of her bag and started lacing one on. No wonder her bag looked so bulky.

Brynn was down on the sidewalk, squinting out at Ocean Drive, as if searching for somebody. "Don't pay her no nevermind," Summer said. "You don't have a big butt. She's just playing. Truth is, Brynn ain't bad, really, once you get to know her. Aw, sugar and spice!"

"What's wrong?"

"Forgot my sunglasses. Wait here for me, 'kay?" Summer clumped carefully up the steps in her blades, gliding past the NO ROLLERBLADES sign and on into the hotel. I'd noticed she was very spacey, always leaving something after castings and having to go back in and get it. I took out *Wuthering Heights* and started to read.

A ridiculously loud Harley pulled up, breaking my concentration. The driver had cornrows and a T-shirt with the sleeves cut off, probably to show off his tattoos. Brynn hoisted up the hem of her dress and climbed onto the back. She took the apple he handed her over his shoulder, and I heard him say, "Here's your lunch, biatch," just before they roared away.

That had to be Loco Luca, Brynn's party promoter boyfriend. Miguel had warned me about him. *He's one slim shady. Stay away, Allee girl.* Luca never came to the apartment. Brynn always met him out somewhere. What was she doing with that dirtbag? He was right about her being a biatch, but she was so hot she could have anybody. This guy, with his hooded eyes and that nose that looked like it had been broken a few times, looked like a lizard.

And that apple couldn't be her whole lunch. Come to think of it, I never saw Brynn eating. Hmmm.

The thought of that apple made my stomach bark (it was way past the growling stage). I'd only had a fat-free blueberry muffin, a cup of coffee, two Nutri-Grain bars, and a water bottle all day, and it was three o'clock. I was exhausted. And hungry. And irritated, which is what I get when I'm exhausted and hungry.

"Allee!" It was Summer, bursting out of the hotel doors on her Rollerblades. She made it down the steps, BlackBerry in hand. "Guess what? I just heard some girls from Irene Marie talking about a casting for *Dietra* magazine this afternoon, so I called the agency and they're gonna go ahead and try to get us in on it."

Another casting? I didn't think so. It wasn't on my to-do list for today, and besides, my feet insisted I get off this insane casting train. "You go. I can't deal with another casting."

She gave me her you've-lost-your-cotton-pickin'-mind look. "Allee. This is *Dietra*! Uta Scholes is shooting it."

"Okay, I don't know what or who that is, but I'm tired, I'm hungry, and I'm finished. Besides, my butt's too big, apparently."

"It's a German magazine, high fashion, real big over there, like *Moda* is in Italy. I reckon it'll pay beans, but the tear sheets'll be great for our books. And you need tears real bad. And it's Uta Scholes. She's the hottest photographer around right now. Been hearin' her name a lot."

"Not happening." I yawned. "Stick a fork in me. I'm done."

Now Summer was yawning. Yawns are always contagious. "I hear ya. I didn't leave the club till three last night. I'm dawg-tired too, but I ain't missin' a *Dietra* casting. Might be for the cover. Oh, and Uta Scholes is a woman." She waited for me to stand up and cheer. Which I would have done if I wasn't so wiped. "Been wantin' to meet her."

"Forget it, Summer. Dimitri told me I'm not right for high fashion anyway. I'm in the commercial division and besides, it's not going to make any difference on my chart if I go to another casting today or not."

"With that attitude it won't. You gotta stay positive. You'll get there. Just 'cause there's a goalie don't mean you can't score." Summer liked to go all motivational speaker-ish on me. Some people were born sunny-side up, like flight attendants. "Let's go home and nap before the casting. Claudette should be back from that Jose Cuervo job today. She might even be at our place by now."

So I'd finally get to meet Claudette. I was curious about her, but I wanted to finish this chapter of *Wuthering Heights*. Cathy's ghost was driving Heathcliff mental, and I loved this part. "I'll meet you there in a little while."

"Cool," she said, vacant-eyed. "I'll see ya back home. Love ya." And she was off, rolling across the street.

Bzzt, bzzt. My BlackBerry was vibrating.

From: Dimitri@FinesseMiami

To: Alleecat1

Subject: Dietra mag/editorial go-see

Editorial casting at the Raleigh hotel, 5:00 TODAY. 150/day, 2-day booking. Six-page spread. Photographer is Uta Scholes. Wants young, innocent, fun look, playful. Commercial types who can cross over and be edgy too. Bathing suit under casual clothes. Natural hair and makeup, go soft-looking.

From: Alleecat1

To: Dimitri@FinesseMiami

Subject: Dietra casting

Any chance I can skip this one? I've been on a lot of castings today and I'm really tired.

From: Dimitri@FinesseMiami

To: Alleecat1

Subject: SKIP THIS ONE???

ARE YOU CRAZY? This is a major editorial casting, every model in town wants to be seen by Uta Scholes, and you think you can just "skip it" BECAUSE YOU'RE TIRED??!! YOU DON'T KNOW THE MEANING OF TIRED! You want to model, you better learn to function at 100% with no sleep. Go have an espresso and don't let me EVER hear you complain about being tired again. Be there at five SHARP, look beautiful, and charm Uta. You can do it. You're fabulous. Kisses, ☺ Dimitri

• • •

Uta Scholes was nothing like the Elmo-hair/Pirate Man duo. Khaki shorts, loose T-shirt, Birkenstocks, she was more like a minivan mom than a fashion client. We were in the Raleigh hotel's conference room at a shiny table scattered with clipboards, an agenda book, a laptop, and a pile of model comps. Mine was on top.

"Relax, you're adorable." Her German accent was so strong it took me a second to figure out what she was saying. And it wasn't easy to relax, since I'd just had a four-dollar coffee. She speed-dialed through my book, flipped it shut, and slid it back to me. I knew this casting was a lost cause. While she was looking, I had a sudden, horrible thought.

What if my model-for-tuition plan was a lost cause? What if I wasted months here and ended up right back where I started, back home at Wal-Mart with no funds for Yale, with everybody in Comet knowing I failed?

"What's wrong?" she asked me.

"What?"

"You look upset."

"Oh, no, I'm fine." *Come on, Allee. Activate fake grin.* "Just thinking about something, that's all."

"Give me scared," she said.

"Give you what?"

"Scared. You just did upset, now pretend you're scared."

Oh, I got it. She wanted expressions. No problem. I bugged out my eyes in terror, like Godzilla was coming right at me.

"No, no, no, not like a cartoon. Think about something that really, truly scares you." Okay, well, there was death. And roller-

91

coasters. Thrill rides didn't thrill me. But there was only one thing that really, truly scared me, more than big, crunchy insects, more than that horrible toenail fungus commercial where they showed the bacteria.

What really, truly scared me was the fear that, twenty years from now, I'd still be in Cape Comet at some dead-end job, sitting in a cubicle staring at a computer screen all day, a nobody, a coulda-woulda-shoulda-been-a-great-somebody. What if I never got to Yale, never accomplished anything really great with my life, and this is my peak? I broke into a cold sweat whenever I thought about that possibility, the possibility of forever being . . . ordinary.

"Good job, Allee. Now give me sweet."

It took me a sec to shake off the willies of doom. "What do you mean, sweet?"

"You know, sweet. Like Glinda the Good Witch."

I batted my eyes and tried a sugary smile, then stopped. "I don't know if I have Glinda in me. I always liked the bad witch better, the green one."

She chuckled. "Why?"

"She got to drive a broom, hang out with flying monkeys, and live in a castle. Way more interesting."

"But she was evil."

"Misunderstood," I said. "Like the Hulk."

"Sounds like you saw this Broadway show *Wicked*," she said.

"I wish. I've never been to a real play. I mean, I've been to plays at the community theater back home, but not one with professional actors."

"Is that right?" she asked.

"Yeah. To be honest, I've never even been to New York. I

read *Wicked*, though. Did you know the play was based on the book?"

"No," she said. "I didn't even know there was a book." She leaned back in her chair, crossed her arms. Maybe she thought I was lying about reading the book. I doubted models read a lot. "You like books?"

I nodded. "I read all the time."

"But what do you do for a good time? Are you hitting all the clubs like a good little model?"

"No. I can't go to clubs. I'm not twenty-one."

"Then what do you do at night?"

I shrugged. "Study for my online classes, e-mail, read."

"You mean to tell me you don't drink?"

"Not really. I think beer tastes like hot dog water."

She threw back her head with a big, hearty laugh. "Hot dog water, *ya*, that's exactly what it tastes like. I'm probably the only German who doesn't like beer. Do you smoke?"

I wrinkled up my nose. "No."

"And you're not much of a drinker. Let me guess. You belong to this, uh, Models for Christ, right?"

"Never heard of it."

"You must be from a little village, then."

"Bingo."

She asked me a lot of questions about myself and Cape Comet, and I was so pathetically grateful she wasn't in a hurry to get rid of me, like clients usually were after they saw my book. It was actually nice to talk to an adult about stuff besides modeling. She almost seemed like a teacher, the kind that liked to hang out with students after class. This didn't even feel like a casting.

The door swung open and Summer walked in, stopping short when she saw us. "Oh, sorry! I didn't think y'all would still be here."

"What did you forget?" I asked.

"Um, this." She took her agenda book off the table, then tip-toed backward, whispering, "Sorry to interrupt, y'all. Love ya," and she was gone. Uta took another look at my book, slower this time. She told me about the shoot that she and the art director for *Dietra* were planning, and that was when I knew, *knew* I had to book this job.

It was an Alice in Wonderland fashion story. *Alice in Wonderland!* That had to mean something, didn't it? The very book I was reading to Robby when I left home. My all-time fave. This had to be fate. I told her all about how much I loved that story.

But she must have thought I was full of it and just telling her all that to get the job, because she answered by saying, "I'll be in touch with the agency," in the same flat way I'd heard all the other clients say it. Maybe fate was playing a practical joke on me. Now I kinda felt like an idiot for going on and on about how much I loved Alice.

Still, Uta Scholes was the nicest client I'd met. No wonder every model in town wanted to be seen by her. It wasn't just because she was the photographer booking models for a major magazine. It was because she treated models like people.

Uta, book me please book me please book me pleaseplease-pleasepleaseplease . . .

chapter 11

So this was Claudette. African-American, long and lean. And super-sexy. I was on the futon, balancing my laptop on my knees, with my books and papers next to me, trying to work on my AP World Lit paper. But I wasn't getting much work done. My eyes kept roaming to Claudette sashaying all over the room. From every pore of maple syrup skin to every corkscrew curl framing her face, she was the sexiest girl I'd ever seen. She was twenty-one, and the way she moved and talked made her seem *über*-sophisticated, like she was living a life of hopping jet planes and popping champagne bottles. Except she was holding this stuffed bear. She hadn't put it down since she got here. And I couldn't get over the barely-there dress she had on. It had to be a nightie she was just passing off as a dress. I was trying not to stare, but I got the feeling she wanted me to, wanted everyone to.

It was practically impossible to concentrate on school stuff with Claudette distracting me. Brynn and Summer were side-tracking me too, talking and getting ready to go out. *I should just give up tonight*, I thought, taking a sip of my orange juice. I was pretty sure Brynn was coming down with a cold or something and I didn't want to catch it. She'd been sniffing a lot.

And Brynn was always in the bathroom. I didn't know what she did in there, except when she was using laxatives, and then, *ew*, unfortunately, we all knew what she was doing in there. Summer was in the bathroom now. She had the door open so she could still talk to everybody while she unraveled the twisty curlers in her hair. "Lord have mercy, Claudette, what are you wearin'?"

"It's a Vittoria Vega. Isn't it fabulosity?"

"Your whole cooter's hangin' out."

"What else is new?" said Brynn, pulling on her Abercrombie ALL ABOUT FUN shirt. "We're lucky Claudie's got underwear on."

"That's underwear?" I asked. "I thought it was a shoestring."

Claudette sat next to me and played with my hair. "You have great hair."

"Thanks." She was very touchy-feely. It was a little bizarre. She had hugged me the second we met.

"Allee, have you met Mars?" she asked, taking the laptop right off my knees and setting it down on the coffee table. She lay down on the futon, throwing her legs over my lap. "Say hello to Mars." She wiggled the stuffed bear at me.

My textbook and all my papers slowly slid to the floor. Great.

96

I had those organized into specific piles. Couldn't she see I was in the middle of something? "Nice bear," I said. "Is that Mars?"

"Yes," she said, hugging it to her. "Mars is my—"

"Home planet," Brynn interrupted, swiping the bear out of her hand. "It's where you're from, you friggin' fruitcake."

Brynn waggled Mars over Claudette's head, then ran into the kitchen with it. Claudette jumped up from the futon, shouting, "Gimme Mars! Gimme!" and she smacked Brynn in the butt.

"Ouch! Hey, hands off, you lezzie." Brynn laughed.

Lezzie? I guessed Claudette was gay. Which was totally fine. I was completely comfortable with lesbians, not that I'd ever met any that I knew of, unless you counted the time I got Rosie O'Donnell's autograph at Disney World. But I just knew I was comfortable with them. Although was she hitting on me with her legs in my lap? Because I'd have to tell her I didn't play for her team.

Brynn tossed Summer the bear, Summer tossed it to me, and I tossed it back to Brynn, who plopped down on the floor in front of me, landing on my notes and crumpling them. Then Claudette did the same thing, sitting cross-legged next to her. Brynn tossed her the precious Mars bear. "Glad you're home, Claudie. Yale here is no fun. Total buzzkill."

No fun. Buzzkill. I hated having that rep. It was like The Fluff calling me *Miss Overachiever* or Hillary High Beams and her *You're always so, like, Queen Serious.* Why did everybody have to label me?

"Brynn, you be nice now, ya hear?" Summer pointed at her with an eyelash curler. "Don't pick on Allee just 'cause she don't party with us."

"Who, me?" Brynn fluttered her eyes and imitated Summer's accent. "Why, Ah wouldn't dream of picking on sweet, little ol' Allee."

Exactly why was fun the end-all, be-all Holy Grail to these people anyway? Their kind of "fun" was the show-offy kind, the club-name-dropping, party-till-you-puke kind. More like pretentious, shallow BS than actual fun. I yanked my papers up from under Brynn's rear end. She didn't even bother to move. One page ripped. Okay, that was it. "You know, you guys go club-hopping every night so you can drink and smoke and grind on the dance floor with guys you don't even know, just so you can get no sleep and wake up hungover and barfing."

"So?" Brynn said.

"That's supposed to be fun?" I asked.

"Hell, yeah!" she yelled.

"What is the point?"

"The point?" Brynn grinned as if I'd said something funny.

"Yeah. The point."

"The point, Allee bo ballee, is that you're so uptight you're not capable of having fun. That's the point. I don't think you could have fun if we paid you."

"Oh, yeah?"

"Yeah."

"That's what you think."

"That's what everybody thinks," she said. Did they? Well, what did they know? I had all kinds of fun, it just didn't involve stupidity. Tomorrow, for my birthday, which none of them knew about because I didn't feel like telling them, I planned to buy myself a book at Murder on the Beach bookstore and have an Oreo/read fest in the afternoon. I really didn't care what Brynn or any of them thought.

Okay, that was a lie.

Because the sad fact was, I shouldn't care, but I did. And it bothered me that I cared, because my mother constantly worried about what other people thought, and it really bugged me, so I tried not to be like that. But I couldn't stand them thinking that I was boring. Dull. Who wanted to be called that? Nobody. "I'm fun," I said, sounding weak, even to myself. "I just have a different idea of what fun is compared to you guys."

"Yeah, glued to your books or computer," Brynn said. "You're a barrel of laughs."

I pretended to read my notes, hiding my face behind my sheet of long hair so they couldn't see how wet my eyes were getting, how red my nose must have been.

Brynn lit a cigarette, blew a smoke ring, and announced to no one in general, "Man, I was so sick at my booking this morning, I don't know how I got through it. Too many Jell-O shots last night."

"Be careful with them Jell-O shots," said Summer. "They got sugar. Tell ya what, you gonna wake up the next day with a belly."

Brynn said, "I just have a salad with balsamic vinegar. The balsamic's a diuretic, so's you pee it all out."

I swear, they couldn't have one conversation without it turning to diet or weight. Now Claudette was lighting one too, leaving me no choice but to crank open the jalousie windows before their smoke took over the room. Brynn and Claudette slipped each other a *look*. "Just trying to prevent cancer," I said, sitting back on the futon, hating myself for saying it, hating myself for sounding exactly like the dull boring bore they thought I was.

Brynn rolled her eyes and opened my World Lit textbook to a picture of Shakespeare. "Who's that drag queen?"

"The Bard," Claudette answered, totally surprising me.

"The what?" Brynn asked.

"Wasn't The Bard married to Janet Jackson?" asked Summer.

"Naw, that's DeBarge," said Brynn. "Saw it on VH1."

"Whatever."

"The Bard is William Shakespeare, you maroons," said Claudette.

"What do you know about Shakespeare?" I asked her.

"I was an English major in college. Only lasted one semester, but I can help you with that paper if you want."

Help me? Now that was funny. "Thanks, I got it covered. What school did you go to?"

"Georgetown."

"In D.C.?"

"Mm-hmm, that's where I'm from."

I wanted to ask her why someone with her intelligence was wasting it here and was she planning on going back to college? Georgetown was a good school. The closest I came to asking what I wanted to ask was, "Why are you modeling?"

She looked at me funny, hesitating for a few seconds. "Sounds like something my father would ask me." She stretched and gave me a big, Cheshire cat smile. "Because I can. And because modeling lets me express myself. I believe in showing my fabulosity at all times. Show your fabulosity, that's my motto."

The phone rang. Summer bolted out of the bathroom to answer it. "Hello? Hey, Dimitri." She brightened up with a big smile, as if he was in the room. "Oh, good. Brynn, me, and you are on option for Monday and Tuesday for that catalog."

"What's the rate?" Brynn asked.

"Two. But we gotta keep it quiet 'cause other agencies are only gettin' fifteen hundred for their girls."

So if their options didn't get dropped, they were going to get booked for two full days. That was four thousand dollars. Elmohair wanted them, but not me. Not one client had wanted me. My passport came in the mail today, another reminder I was supposed to be traveling, working, making big bucks.

Hello, depression. A wave of it washed over me, crashing down to my toes. I couldn't wait for them to leave so I could swim in it.

It must have shown on my face, because Summer said into the phone, "So, Dimitri, anything for Allee? . . . You're expecting lots of TV castings for her next week? Okay, I'll tell her. Love ya." She hung up and went back to the bathroom mirror, finger-combing waxy ringlets all over her head. "Allee, it looked like you and Uta Scholes were gettin' on like peas and carrots. She might book you." Just hearing Uta's name made my insides flutter. I wanted that booking so badly it hurt my bones.

"Stop blowing sunshine up her ass, Summer," Brynn said. "Uta's looking for Alice in Wonderland. Allee's not even blond. Uta's gonna book you."

"You never know," said Summer. "Although she did want commercial types who could cross over and be edgy and I'll tell ya what, that's me. I'm commercial and fashion, but Allee, you're jest mostly commercial." How did she know this? Was there some kind of index somewhere with our pictures on it and labels underneath that said "commercial" or "fashion"?

Summer walked over to the kitchen, opened the cabinet over the stove, the one full of hair accessories, and pulled out a blue headband. "Uta said she wants an Alice with a twist. Looky here, do I look like Alice?" She put it on and I realized, with a sinking heart, that she looked like the most beautiful Alice I'd ever seen, straight out of the storybook. I wanted to punch her stupid, Alice-y face.

Claudette jumped up off the floor and snatched the headband off, messing up some of Summer's curls. "Hey!" Summer shouted.

Claudette crowned herself with the headband like it was a tiara. "If she wants Alice with a twist, then she shouldn't go with the same old vanilla. Everybody prefers chocolate, you know."

Summer tugged the headband off Claudette and put it back on herself. "Ludacris didn't want no chocolate. I got booked for his video tomorrow."

"Hey, Claudie, why didn't you get that?" Brynn asked.

"I'm probably not black enough. That's what BET told Momma when she sent my reel to them for that VJ gig. It doesn't matter for print that I'm mixed, but for TV they always want you to fit into a type."

Summer tossed the headband on the floor. It landed on a pile of shoes and magazines. "Don't that suck about TV? I'm a killer actress. And I don't get near enough acting auditions because I don't fit into the type they're lookin' for. It ain't fair."

Claudette flounced onto the futon. "You'll still be the token white girl at that video job tomorrow, you know."

"I'll still get to meet Ludacris and make five hundred. Call time's at seven-thirty, so I'm jest goin' out tonight for an hour."

"Why go at all?" I asked.

"I found out photographers from all the local magazines'll be at the club tonight—*Ocean Drive*, *D'Luxe*. Clients too."

"How do you always know stuff like that?" Brynn asked. "I swear, Summer, you got more inside scoop than Luca, and he knows everyone on the beach." Summer didn't answer, just gave her a close-lipped smile. I could tell it irritated Brynn. "So tell us, Miss FBI, where are Vodka and Tonic these days?"

"I heard the DeWalt Hotel paid 'em fifty bucks just to sit at the bar in their new restaurant, you know, to dress up the place. The owner saw them two on the street and offered 'em cash."

Nobody said anything for a few minutes. I guess we were all thinking how scary it must be to hit the lowest rung of modeling, if you'd even call that modeling. Summer poured water into the nearly empty hand soap container. She did cheap stuff like that, like brush her teeth with baking soda instead of toothpaste. Here was a girl who spent five hundred bucks on a pair of Manolo Ballnicks or whatever-his-name-is, paid a ton for some big-deal personal trainer to the stars, and yet I was pretty sure she'd used the same paper cup since I'd gotten here. Weirdness.

The phone was ringing again. Summer raced across the room to pick it up. She had a thing about the phone, never gave anybody else a chance to get it. "Hello? . . . I shoulda known it was you, ma'am. It's ten o'clock, right on time. . . . Yes, ma'am, she's right here."

Summer handed the phone to Brynn, who said, "Hi, Ma." Tonight it was a short conversation. After Brynn yelled at her mother for not keeping a doctor's appointment and used language I couldn't believe anyone would use with their mother, she hung up.

"You know what, Allee, you really should come out with us for once," Summer said. She was back at the bathroom sink, brushing hair dye onto her eyebrows. "We're going to Dali tonight. The music's great and the bartenders are all, whatchamacallit, dwarfs. Don't tell me they have that in Cape Rocket."

"Comet. Did you say—"

"Little people," said Claudette. "Dwarfs. Wearing lederhosen."

That was so awful I didn't even know what to say except "Why?"

"I don't know, but they make a buttload in tips," said Brynn, pulling on a pair of stretch skinny jeans. "So. You coming to see for yourself or what?"

Rather than ask why I would ever want to see anything so sick, I just got out of it with "I can't. I don't have a fake ID." They all bounced glances off each other.

Brynn used a voice you'd use with a four-year-old: "You don't need a fake ID. You're a model."

"But—"

"There ain't one velvet rope you have to wait at," Summer said. "And most of 'em card at the bar, not the door. But you can use my fake ID if you want. They never look at the picture."

"No, thanks. I won't be able to relax anyway, not till I get this assignment done. I have to e-mail it to my teacher by Monday."

"Fa Christ's sake, you got the whole weekend," Brynn said.

Claudette waved Mars at me. "Come on. Mars says it's Friday night."

I shook my head no. The big, fat, real reason I didn't want to go out with them was that I didn't have the right clothes. I'd seen what they wore to those clubs, and I didn't have anything even close. And I wasn't comfortable asking any of them if I could borrow something. Plus I wasn't a drinker. I'd never be able to keep up with them. And I was here to save money, not blow it at clubs and restaurants. That was the best excuse I could give them. "I'm on a budget right now. I'm trying to save money."

"Champagne in the VIP room is free," said Summer. "And if you're with us, you ain't payin' no cover charge."

"Thanks, but I don't think so." To change the subject, I asked Claudette, "How was your Jose Cuervo booking?"

"Amazing," she said. "The director was so nice. I really hope I get to work with him again."

"Is Jose the director?" I ask.

"What?" She looked confused.

"Jose Cuervo. Is he the director?"

There was about three seconds of silence before the three of them were doubled over laughing. Brynn was rolling around on the floor, choking on her cigarette. Something told me Jose Cuervo was not a director.

"You d-don't know wh-what Jose Cuervo is?" Claudette sputtered, trying to get her hysterics under control.

I shrugged, grinned hopefully. "A client?"

Claudette bopped over to her still-packed suitcase in the middle of the floor and pulled out a bottle with the words *Jose Cuervo* swirling all over it. I could feel my face falling. A prickly heat was spreading along my arms, up to my head. "Here you go, here's the client, Allee."

"Hey, Allee," said Brynn. "Did I tell you tomorrow Lucky the Leprechaun is directing me in a Lucky Charms commercial?" Screams of laughter. "Yeah, I'd love to work with him again. He's magically delicious." More shrieks and clutching of stomachs. When it died down, Brynn pointed at me and added, "Not exactly a rocket scientist, is she?"

"My dad's a rocket scientist," I said.

Brynn bolted straight up. "Wait a friggin' second. You mean to tell me you're from Cape Comet and your dad is a rocket scientist?" I nodded.

Explosive, supernova of hilarity. All over again.

I guess it did sound kind of goofy. A rocket scientist from Cape Comet. Gee, I'd never thought about it before. A giggle burbled up and out of me, and then another one and another one. It was like that day at school in the hall with the toilet paper. I looked over at Summer. Her eyebrows looked like furry spaghettis with all that gooey dye on them. It cracked me up even more. We were all laughing together now. And it felt nice, like I'd made some kind of connection with all of them, even Brynn.

chapter 12

Finally, I was finished cleaning. Every night my routine was to straighten up the whole apartment after they left to go clubbing. The mess in here was like static on the radio or a kid crying at the movies: just plain annoying.

The nights were the hardest here. I was always alone after everyone went out, and I still wasn't used to it. It made me feel as empty as this apartment. At home, I'd always had my sister to talk to at night, ever since we were little. Even if we weren't exactly talking, like in the week before I left, I still saw her, or felt her next to me, in bed or in her closet, trying on clothes. I'd sent her a few e-mails, but she hadn't written me back. She hadn't called either.

I turned on the TV. David Letterman would get my mind off The Fluff. I got into my new cozy Yale pajamas, a birthday present from my parents, and stepped up onto Summer's bed with her pink ruffly comforter covered in clothes and magazines, then hoisted myself up to my bed, stretched out, and pulled out *Wuthering Heights* from under my pillow.

Rat, tata tat tat. Tat tat. Who was knocking at the door at this hour? *Letterman* was starting. *Rat, tata tat tat. Tat tat.* I looked through the peephole. It was Miguel. His voice went right through the door. "Shello, care to go shopping?"

I opened it and he darted in. He kissed me hello. "It's so late," I told him. "What are you doing here?"

"My fake-Gucci-sunglasses-wearing, trying-to-pass-for-Cuban-but-everybody-knows-he's-really-Puerto Rican, *hijo-de-puta* date canceled on me. But I'm not bitter. Care to join me for some retail therapy?"

"Now?"

"*Sí.*"

"I'm in bed." I laughed. "Are you crazy? It's after eleven."

"That's the best time."

"Are stores even open now?"

"Of course. New York isn't the city that never sleeps, you know. It's SoBe."

"Miguel, I can't go shopping now." '

"Yes, you can. Right after you walk on my back."

This guy didn't take no for an answer. "Miguel, can we go tomorrow? I know I need clothes for castings, but I'm just so tired."

"Okay, get some rest, Sleeping Beauty. Or should I say Alice?

I'll light a candle for you so you get that editorial." He kissed my cheek, started to walk out.

"Wait. Why don't you watch *Letterman* with me and share my dinner? It's just dry Cheerios, but they're honey nut." I suddenly really wanted him to stay. "Please, stay. You're the only person who won't make me feel crappy for eating carbs at night. And in a few minutes, it'll officially be my birthday."

"What? Why didn't you say so?" he said, giving me a big hug and helping himself to a Cheerio. "We need to celebrate! But walk on my back first. You know you love hearing it crack."

I had to admit, it did give me a sick thrill.

"Tell me about your family," he said while I stood on his spine.

"My dad works for the space program. He's really smart. Well, with everything except my college fund. That, he kinda messed up."

"*Ay*, move up an inch. That's good. What about your mom?"

Heavy sigh. "We're not so alike. She's more like my sister, Sabrina."

"What's Sabrina like?"

"Let's just say, she's not exactly headed for Yale. She reads magazines, not books. We're very different. But close, kinda, just not right now. She's not speaking to me."

"Why? What happened?"

I sighed again. "Sabrina was supposed to be the model, not me. I stole her dream."

"Then maybe that's all it was," Miguel said. "A dream. And maybe you're the real thing, you ever think of that?"

"I don't know. She's just like my mother. Mom wants me

to be another Sabrina. Or another her. Into heels and skirts and girly stuff."

"So what's wrong with that?"

"Nothing, but she doesn't get that I couldn't care less if my nails are bitten or my ponytail is messy. It's not that I don't *like* having a good hair day, it's just that I don't think my world *revolves around* a good hair day, or the latest designer jeans, like they do. I have other priorities."

"Like getting to Yale."

"How'd you know?"

"It's all over your pajamas. What do you want to major in?"

"English literature. Nineteenth-century women writers, mainly. You know, Emily Brontë, Jane Austen, Mary Shelley."

Miguel fake-snored. I gave him a gentle kick with my heel. He pretended to wake up and said, "Which one of those writers is the one Nicole Kidman played in that movie, you know, where she had the big fake nose and she wrote stories and then killed herself?"

"None." I laughed. "That was Virginia Woolf. Different time period."

"Or how about the one with Gwyneth Paltrow? Same story. She writes, she cries a lot, she kills herself. Ooh, but her husband was really cute in that one."

"That was Sylvia Plath."

"What do you need to go to Yale for? You already know everything. *Yo sé*. I know. You're trying to prove you're more than a pretty face, *verdad*?"

I shrugged. "I want to be more than my sister or my mom are

ever going to be, that's for sure." I gave him another little kick. "And besides, I already am more than a pretty face."

"So am I. So are most people, when you get to know them. *Ay*, your feet are magic. Go down a little, Allee." I moved a few inches down his back. "Right there, that's good. So, what are you going to do after Yale?"

"Get a Ph.D. maybe. Become Dr. Allee Rosen, Yale professor. Write books, teach, be a big name in academia."

"Where? You're not going to get one of those horrible tweed jackets with patches on the elbows, are you? That's why all those writers killed themselves, you know. If they'd had better clothes they wouldn't have been thinking about death all the time."

"Interesting theory."

"It's true. Clothes affect your emotions. And maybe you and your mom have different priorities, but you know what? I got a feeling you might *like* heels and accessories and girly stuff."

"I doubt it."

"Don't knock it till you try it, *niña*. I was Catwoman for Halloween once and I worked those stiletto boots better than Halle Berry. Truth."

Miguel was late. He said he'd take me shopping last night, but I was starting to think maybe he'd forgotten. I was outside on the sidewalk, waiting for him.

My BlackBerry was ringing. "Hello."

"Happy birthday!"

"Hi, Mom."

"Hi, honey. I can't believe you're seventeen! I thought maybe you'd come home for your birthday, surprise us. But you didn't. I got a cake and everything."

"Mom, they have castings on Saturdays and Sundays. I can't leave."

"What about during the week?"

"Mom . . ."

"I want to see you. Are you dressing up more? What jewelry are you wearing?"

"None. But I'm thinking about getting a nose ring."

"Maybe Dad and I will come down and make sure you're taking care of yourself."

"Yes, because I am totally incapable of taking care of myself. Did I tell you I left the refrigerator open all day?"

"Allee—"

"Because I forgot to close it when I drank directly from the milk container, after running through the apartment with scissors."

"Has anyone offered you drugs?"

"Yes, a carb burner. Listen, is Sabrina there?"

I heard Mom yell, "Sabrina! Sabrina!" Then muffled whispering, the slam of a door. Mom got back on the phone.

"She doesn't want to talk to you, Allee. I'm sorry, honey. I've tried to get her to call you, but she's not ready, I guess."

"God, she needs get over it already."

"I know, Allee, but it's very hard for her with you out there, getting to do what she wants to do so badly. Put yourself in her shoes."

Way to go with the guilt trip, Mom.

I heard the clicking sound of another person on the line. "Happy barf day." It was my sister. I waited for her to say something else. She didn't. We just listened to each other breathing until we heard the *click* of Mom hanging up.

"So . . . are you going to apologize for the way you acted?" I asked.

"Do you want me to send you my Heidi Klum book about modeling?"

"I accept your apology."

"I'm not apologizing. You should be apologizing. You're the one who screwed up my audition with your babyish tantrum in front of the scouts!" she yelled.

"Yeah, because you never told me about the phone call!" I yelled back, scaring a stray cat into the bushes. "It's all your fault!"

"It is not!"

"It is too!"

"Is not!"

"Is too!"

"Fine! I'm sorry!"

Excuse me. What just happened?

That was definitely an apology. So I said, "Okay, fine. I'm sorry too."

We listened to each other breathe again, and then she said, "So, how are you doing there?"

"Okay, I guess."

"Have you gone out for any fashion mags?"

"Yeah. For this one German magazine, *Dietra.*"

"That is super-high fashion. Did you get it?"

"It's really competitive, Sabrina. Like, way worse than I thought."

"Really? Well . . . just, you know, think positive. Like, let the competition worry about the competition. That's what you said when you applied to Yale."

"That was different."

"I wonder what clothes you'd get to wear for *Dietra*. You might have to show some skin."

"What do you mean, show some skin?"

"Allee, have you ever looked at high-fashion magazines? All the models are, like, half naked and freaky-looking. Even the famous ones like Kate Moss. Who's the photographer? Anyone big?"

"Kinda. Uta Scholes. Do you know her?"

"Omigod! I've seen her photos online. Watch, you'll get this one, even though I still say you're so not model material."

"Thanks for your support. I think."

Her voice softened. "Hey, I'm not mad anymore. And if I can't be the one in magazines, then I guess I'm glad it's you, even if you are a total loser with no fashion sense, like, whatsoever."

That was so sweet. "Thanks," I said, getting all choked up.

"Okay, so happy barf day. Here's Dad."

Everything felt right again, me being back to normal with her. It felt like nothing had happened between us, like we'd just spoken yesterday or something. Maybe it was a sign things were looking up. Maybe my luck was going to change.

I heard the crackly sound of the phone being passed. "Happy birthday!"

"Hi, Dad."

"So, is your modeling career taking off yet?"

"Dad, that is not helpful." He knew my career wasn't taking off. My parents called me every other day.

He cleared his throat. "Listen, I, uh, spoke to Monique and Momma the other day."

"You did?"

"Yeah, I just wanted to know what's going on. You've been there almost a month and haven't gotten one lousy job. "

"Again, not helpful."

"Listen, Allee, you're beautiful to me, you know that. Those clients are blind if they don't pick you. But I just think if you're not getting any work, you should come home. I can't see you wasting the rest of your senior year there, not studying or working for the rest of the school year."

"But, Dad—"

"This was never your idea to begin with. Maybe it wasn't meant to be."

"Or maybe it was. And it's about to happen. All I need is a couple of good commercials to make the really big money. And Momma told me I'm great for commercials."

"But if you don't get a commercial this season, then this was all a waste. You have to think about what you're doing for college. You know U of Florida has a good science department. Their business school isn't bad either."

"Dad, you know I want to major in English," I said through gritted teeth. "*At Yale.*"

"I just want you to be realistic," he said. Dad worried that majoring in English wasn't practical and I wouldn't get a high-paying job in the future. But I really didn't want to study anything else. He was always hinting that I follow in his footsteps or go into the corporate world. Yuck.

"Two more weeks, Allee. That's it. If you don't get any work by then, you're coming home."

AAAAAAHHH!!! Every time I thought about what Dad had said, panic gripped my throat like a python squeezing it and I had to stop and force myself to calm down and breathe.

I could not, could not, *could not* go home. I just couldn't. Everyone was going to say I was a loser. A joke. I'd be pointed at, laughed at, ridiculed. *"Imagine, Allee Rosen telling everybody she was modeling when she wasn't."* Going home was NOT an option.

"Allee, you don't have to make that face. They don't look that bad. Turn around again." Miguel and I were at a vintage store, the last stop on Miguel's shopping hit parade. Summer had told me he loved vintage stores. I invited her to come along, but she had a session with her trainer.

Miguel had already taken me to Chroma and Lavish and a few other expensive boutiques just for browsing and celebrity-hunting (we saw Nicole Richie), and then we went to Urban Outfitters and a few other stores for serious purchasing. So far, I'd bought some bright-colored minidresses, some tops, belts, and a rhinestone gun "to give your current wardrobe a little za-za-fritz." Now we were looking at jeans. "You know what? You've lost weight, Allee girl. You need a size smaller." He was right. These jeans were hanging on me. All my clothes had gotten really baggy lately. "What diet have you been on?"

"The I-don't-have-time-to-eat diet."

"You're not doing those crazy Brazilian weight-loss pills that are going around, are you? You don't want to get too thin. You're not high fashion, you're a commercial girl."

"No, I would never take pills. Hey, what about those?" I held up another pair of jeans with embroidery on the pockets.

"Nah. Not for you. And the smaller the pocket the bigger your booty looks. But then again, the whole big booty thing is in again now, so I don't know, maybe . . ."

"So, it's true," I groaned. "I do have a big one."

"Yeah, and you'll slam all the Latino castings with that thing. Own it, love it. It's brash, it's brazen, it's saying hello to the world whether you like it or not—or good-bye, depending on which way you're walking, and—"

"It's that big? Even though I lost a couple pounds?"

"Allee. You can't spell 'fantastic' without ass. Just ask J.Lo."

"Um, actually, that's not true. It's f-a-n-t—"

"You're bootay-licious, show it off, girl. In this Marc Jacobs skirt. Wow, it's only forty bucks."

I tried it on. Miguel paired it with a sequined tube top, a big, floppy hat, and a gazillion bangles. When I came out of the fitting room he went, "Bull's-eye. Give me a catalog pose." I put my hand on my hip and stared blankly into the distance. He clapped his hands.

"But, Miguel, this looks like a costume. Real people don't dress like this."

"Real people? Who cares about them? *Pero*, you know what? Maybe that's your problem, worrying about real people. You gotta forget what's real, Allee. Modeling is all about make-believe and dressing up, you know? It's all about fun." Again with the fun. If one more person told me to have fun, I'd shoot them with my rhinestone gun. "Didn't you ever dress up your Barbie? I did. In secret. This is the same thing, except you get to *be* Barbie."

"*Uch*, Barbies give little girls self-esteem issues. No one can look like that. Can't I dress up in something a little more, you know, me?"

"You're not home anymore. You don't have to be the same person you are at home. But, okay, let's go a different way." The next outfit he put together was a cropped cardigan over a snug polo, plaid mini, and little square, blue, plastic glasses (we popped the lenses out). I stepped out of the fitting room and he went, "*Voilà,* the hot nerdy thing still works. This look is great for TV, when they're casting for the high school kid or college kid, except they'll make you lose the glasses so they can see your face better. Wear them on top of your head instead of a headband. You can wear flats with this—loafers or Keds even—but the rest of the time, heels, girl, high heels."

"I can't walk in heels. They make me look like a spaz."

"Have you practiced?"

"No."

"Well, then, what do you expect? Models don't come out of a box with all the moves. Look in the mirror, practice your poses, practice, practice, practice. And wear bright colors, because a life without color is a life without color." He gasped. "Damn, that's good. I need to write that down and save it for when I have my own makeover show on the Style channel." He held up an air microphone. "This is Miguel Sanchez-Garcia signing off, reminding you that a life without color is a life without color." He winked. "Thanks for watching."

Miguel still had to pick out one more outfit, something I could wear to a club. Except I wasn't sure I could trust him on this one. First of all, he insisted we had to get it at this two-story shop called CeeCee Bloom, specializing in clothing and accessories for cross-dressers. Excuse me, but a lot of the clothing in CeeCee Bloom was in the omigod-are-you-kidding-me category, although Abuela would have loved all the wigs, pancake makeup, and feather boas.

"Allee!" Uh-oh. He had something very glittery in his hands. "*Ven aqui.* Try this on."

He handed me an itty-bitty dress. "Miguel, are you sure?" I could just hear Brynn right now, shooting some insult at me, making everyone laugh. What had gotten into me? Why, why, *why* did I care what they thought? I sounded like my mother, worrying what people would say. Or The Fluff, obsessing about clothes. "I'm not sure about this one."

"Stop whining. Just try it on."

The dress was black with silver straps, backless, and very short. It looked great on me, showed off my toned legs and arms. I really liked the way the clingy material, well, clung to me. I felt like a different person in this. I had to give him props. I walked out of the dressing room and Miguel sang, "She's a sexy supah stah . . . bow chicka bow bow . . ."

I smiled. "I never thought I'd say this, but I love it."

"I knew I was right about you. There's a you that you haven't even met yet. Oh, yes, *niña*. There is."

"How do I wear a bra with this?"

"You don't."

"Oh." I didn't know if I could do that. "This is black, though. What about 'a life without color—' "

"Forget the rule at night. It's a daytime rule. And the mini-dress will never go out. It's the little trend that could. *Ay*, Brynn will die of jealousy when she sees you in this, just die." I couldn't help beaming. "It's missing something, though. Here, try this." He took a black leather belt with studs right off the mannequin next to us. He also took off the dog collar. "Don't give me that look. Try them on." I did. And I looked ridiculoso. But Miguel didn't think so. "See? It works. A little bit swank, a little bit spank."

"How about I get the belt, but not the dog collar?"

After a lot of eye-rolling and protesting, he gave up on the dog collar.

I went back to the dressing room to change, and I studied myself in the mirror for a long time. *A new me I haven't met yet.* I wanted to be this person I was looking at, this smiling girl in a great dress. I wasn't a buzzkill, like Brynn said. I'd just never tried to be part of things. They were right that I didn't take part in the fun. It was an old habit, me always being a fly on the wall, never being at the party, just hearing about it later or watching from a distance.

But I didn't want to be the person I was back home anymore. I wanted to be more like Alice. I slowly turned around, looking at myself in the mirror from every angle. *It's all about make-believe* . . . what would Alice do if she were me? She'd not only wear this dress, she'd wear it to the mad tea party and dance all night. Alice didn't hesitate to try new things.

No more clipping my BlackBerry on. Good-bye, Allee. Hello, Alice.

chapter 13

I bought the dress and belt, wondering how I was going to work up the guts to wear it, plus a Che Guevara T-shirt and a gift for my sister, a necklace with purple blue stones, the same color as her eyes. Miguel bought a mauve satin pajama set and matching eye mask that said *Sleeping Beauty*. Then we left and went out onto Lincoln Road, an open-air pedestrian mall of shops, art galleries, and restaurants. We passed Rollerbladers, women with dogs in their purses, Frankenmuscle fitness freaks, stray cats, kids on scooters, business-suit banker types, Euro-backpackers, and a performance artist spitting dried fruit onto a blank canvas. It made me feel alive, being part of this funky human salad.

I really, really, really didn't want to go back to Cape Comet.

"*Qué te pasa, niña?* You seem distracted."

"I don't know if I can pull this off."

"Borrow my attitude and you'll be fine. Isaac Mizrahi says style is all about conviction."

"No, no, not just about the dress. I mean about being a model. Maybe it's not meant to be. That's what my dad said."

"You know what my dad said? My dad said I should be a police officer like my brothers."

I stopped in my tracks and looked down at his ninety-eight-pound frame. "You? A police officer?"

"You heard me."

"Was your dad blind? Deaf? Brainless?"

"All of the above. Come on, I'll tell you about it over lunch. Let's go to the News."

"What's the News?"

"The News Cafe." He put his hand over his heart. "You can get newspapers and magazines from all over the world there *and* a fabulous spinach wrap with goat cheese and pecans. Versace was on his way there to get his morning coffee and paper when he was shot, *Que Dios lo tenga en su gloria.*" He crossed himself.

We sat outside at a little white table with a green umbrella over us. Two bizarre, pudgy old ladies walked by wearing matching yellow suits with black polka dots and matching wide-brimmed hats that were also yellow with black polka dots. They reminded me of Tweedledee and Tweedledum. "The Skull sisters," Miguel said, after they'd strolled by. "Very famous artists. They do 3-D paintings, mostly scenes of Cuba." A black guy in a one-piece green leotard Rollerbladed past us, practically in slow motion. It was like he was barely moving. "We call him the Green Hornet."

A man wearing cargo shorts and a top hat was showing someone a card trick at a nearby table. A mad hatter on the beach? I looked at Miguel. "I don't know him." This place was as surreal as Wonderland, full of bizarre characters. Sometimes when I walked around here, I wasn't sure if I was really seeing what I was seeing.

After lunch, we walked two blocks over to Washington, to have coffee at Kitsch and Dish. The walls were cluttered with metal lunch boxes from the seventies, Cabbage Patch dolls, and other assorted garage sale decor. Our waitress was in her sixties and she was wearing wooden, pink flamingo earrings that kinda blended with her rose-colored beehive. We curled up on two velvet chairs in front of a coffee table topped with Madonna's *Sex* book.

My BlackBerry kept vibrating. I ignored it. It was probably Abuela and Robby with birthday calls, and I wasn't up to doing the whole yippee, it's my birthday thing. I'd check the messages on my voice mail later. Right now I'd rather listen to Miguel telling me all about his horrific high school years with his caveman cop dad and cop brothers. "How did you survive it?" I asked him.

"I knew I'd get out of the house as soon as I could, and that dream kept me going. I've been free for two years now." He sipped his coffee slowly, lost in thought, then put his mug down and did a little shimmy shake. "So that's the 411 on *mi familia*. I survived. But you know what? People can survive anything. It's surviving in great clothes that's the trick."

"You really should have your own show."

"I know." Dramatic gasp. "Don't look, there's the guy who stood me up last night."

"Where?" Of course I looked anyway, but only saw the back of some blond guy.

"Piece of *mierda*. Some men are about as useful as a sleeveless turtleneck." He sipped his coffee. "Okay, so, back to what I was saying. This business attracts survivors, I think, people who've made it through rough times and reinvented themselves, like me."

"Yeah, well, I better reinvent myself pretty soon or I'll be outta here." I told him about Dad's time limit. "I have to start getting booked, Miguel. Like, tomorrow. Seriously. I have to."

"You will, *niña*. You've got the body, the skin, the teeth, your hair is magnif. And now you've got the right clothes. You just need to find your ticket."

"What do you mean, find my ticket?"

"Every model's got a ticket."

"Like what?"

"I'll give you an example. You know that April girl, the one who books every catalog and every magazine but looks like a starving refugee?"

"Yeah. I saw her yesterday."

"Did you notice her eyes?"

"No, but they were probably blah like the rest of her."

"Take a closer look the next time you see her. Her eyes are such a light green they're almost yellow, *te lo juro*, like a golden apple. You can only notice it when she has makeup on. It's amazing to see on film what she can do with them, what she can express. I've seen her book. I'll show it to you. Anyway, her ticket is her eyes."

"So a ticket is like a gimmick."

"No. A gimmick is something you make up, work at, like Summer's dumb blond act."

"Um . . . excuse me, but I don't exactly think that's an act, Miguel. She's not the sharpest knife in the drawer, trust me."

"No, trust *me*, she's dumb all the way to the bank. Gimmicks never last, though, because anyone can have one. Tickets are one of a kind. A ticket is what you already have. A quality only you can wind up and work. It's what makes you stand out. *Entiendes?*"

"Maybe. I'm not sure."

"Okay, there was this one model, Susie M? She's in New York now, but she had the whole package, like you, and she still wasn't getting booked. Then one day she realized she had this dancer's body, graceful, *elegante*, you know? Because she'd had serious ballet training since she was like, in diapers or something. So anyway, her booker set her up with this fantastic photographer and she did these nude shots, really artistic, high-concept, great lighting. Guess what happened after that?

"What?"

"She blew up."

"She got fat?"

"No, *idiota*, her career blew up. She, like, doubled her day rate. Her kind of body was unique, like a sculpture or a Thoroughbred racehorse, so she used it. And that, *mi amor*, was her ticket."

"So what's my ticket?" I couldn't wait to find out.

He sipped his coffee, shook his head. "I don't know, *niña*. That's what you have to find out. So open your eyes, girl. But not too much. It'll give your forehead wrinkles."

Beeep: "Happy birthday, Allee. Mom says to say I love you. I stopped wetting the bed. When are you coming home?"

"No, wait, Robby, it's Abuela's turn, don't hang—" *Click.*

Beeeep: "*Feliz cumpleaños, Allee.* I can't believe you are seventeen now, almost the age I got married. *Dios te bendiga, mi vida*. Did you know I was married at eighteen? And did you know I had to quit my job at Wal-Mart because you weren't here to take me? I could have been a model, you know. Just be careful. It's a doggy doggy world. They all the time want sexy pictures. Allee, don't do it. The pictures will end up on the aquanet and then everyone will say you are a *puta*."

Click.

Another week went by with no work. Just castings. I was more worried than ever about having to go home. I could almost feel the pull of Mom and Dad, sucking me back to Cape Comet. It wasn't that they wanted me to fail. I knew they were proud of me and wanted me to succeed, but I also knew they were insanely overprotective and wanted me close by. If Mom hadn't had Robby to take care of, she probably would have moved to South Beach with me. What would my parents do when I went to Yale?

I was running out of time, so I did some research and came up with a strategy.

My Strategy to Get Work (as pieced together with advice from various experts)
1) Say you'll do anything, and don't worry if it's legal. (Claudette and Brynn)
2) Stop living on granola bars. You're looking worn out. Switch to protein PowerBars. (Everyone)
3) Explore a new side of yourself. Be brave. (Claudette)
4) Never put your contact sheets in the back flap of your book. You don't want clients to see unflattering shots of you, do you? (Miguel)

5) *Let yourelf go freaky-deaky, drop your inhibitions. It'll show in your pix. (Claudette)*

6) *Videotape yourself with nothing on. Watch and learn your best angles. (Claudette)*

7) *Put your schoolbooks down.* Glamour, Elle, Allure, *and* Star *magazine are your textbooks now. Watch E! for extra credit. (Miguel)*

8) *Watch good models working on a shoot and pay attention. (Summer)*

9) *Take an acting workshop. (Everyone)*

10) *Check in at the agency often, especially for TV. You want to remind the agents to push you. (Miguel)*

I told The Fluff all about my shopping trip with Miguel. "You should see the little black dress I got. You'd love it. It is so you."

"I can't see you in a little black dress. Oh, guess what?"

"We're adopted. I knew we weren't related."

"I'm making a lot of clothes now. There's, like, this fashion show at school the Key Club is doing, a benefit for the hurricane victims, and they asked me to sew a few of the pieces. You should see me. I'm sewing till one in the morning every night."

"When are you doing your homework?"

"What are you, Mom?" she shouted.

"Sorry, sorry. That's actually really cool. I wish I could sew."

"I can make you something and send it to you if you want. A dress, maybe. You need clothes."

"Okay." I doubted she was making anything I could wear in South Beach. Cape Comet was so behind the times with cloth-ing. I could really see that now, living here. But she wanted to

127

do something nice for me, and that was cool. "Thanks, that'd be great," I said.

Finances

food (granola bars, cereal, water bottles, Starbucks) ??? approx. $100

rent ??? (varies, depending on how many models are here, to be taken out of my first paycheck)

test shoots $550 (will be taken out of my pay)

entertainment $0 (Romero Britto gallery was free)

portfolio and composite prints $300 (taken out of my first pay)

new clothes $338 (not including $100 Mom and Dad sent for my birthday, so really $438)

Laundromat ??? $20

makeup/toiletries $120

waxing, pedi, and mani $130

Lori Wyman Acting for Commercials Workshop $275

hair trim, hot oil treatment, and blowout $70

DustBuster for vacuuming dropped ashes $50

magazines $22

INCOME: $0

Claudette was at a casting for Dark and Lovely, while Summer, Brynn, and I were at the Ritz-Carlton pool, lying on lounge chairs in bikinis, pretending we were guests. We had snuck in from the beach without going through the lobby. It was Summer's idea. I spotted a couple of other models here, probably doing the same thing. The girls were long-limbed and the guys were all either lanky or built, with shaved chests and perfect abs. There were some families here too, with little kids running around.

I was wearing Claudette's red bikini (the only one that wasn't a thong) that she'd lent me, high-wedge flip-flops, red lipstick, and a red bandanna for a headband.

Alice was in the house.

"Why are we going here when there are so many other pools we could go to?" I asked Summer. "Pools where we don't have to sneak?" I was scared we were gonna get kicked out of here any second. I'm so not a rule-breaker.

"'Cause other pools don't have *him*," Summer answered. I followed her gaze to a dark-haired, Mediterranean-looking guy wearing a T-shirt that said TANNING BUTLER. It was so tight it was straining over his biceps and chest, about to rip open at the seams any minute.

"What's a tanning butler?" I asked.

"I'll show you," said Brynn. "Hey, Jason!" she shouted across the pool, waving. She was chewing her gum cow-style, mouth open, saliva sloshing. "Hey! Over here!" Some sunbathers lifted their heads to see who was making all the noise. We were so getting kicked out of here.

Jason strutted over to us, flashing bleached white teeth. He gave a little bow. "Ladies."

"Hi," all three of us said, our eyes glued to the muscle dance he had going on under that shirt. He was flexing his pecs. UpDownUpDownUpDown. I had this wild urge to laugh.

Brynn handed Jason her suntan lotion and went, "Allee here needs you to rub lotion on her back."

What?! "No, no, no, that's okay," I babbled to Jason. "You don't have to. I mean, thank you, but I don't need you to do that."

"Oh, yeah, you do," Brynn said. She pointed at me with her thumb and said to Jason, "Believe me, this loser needs a friggin' rubdown."

"Shoot, Brynn, leave her alone," Summer said. "Allee's only seventeen." Like she was so much older, at eighteen. Still, I was grateful she was sticking up for me like she always did.

I wanted to get Brynn back. This was what I came up with: "Who are you calling a loser? You're a loser." *Omigod, I was so lame.*

"I know you are but what am I?" said Brynn, mocking my lameness. Jason just stood there. His pecs started doing the hokey-pokey again. And that urge to laugh came back. Brynn felt it too. I could tell.

"Uh, you ladies want me to come back?" he asked. Up, down, up down, flex, flex, flex. I couldn't take it. I clamped my hand over my mouth like a lid and laughed into it. Brynn looked away, but I could see her shoulders shaking with laughter.

Summer just winked up at him and went, "You can go ahead and put that lotion on my back. And 'scuse these two. They weren't raised right." And then she rolled over onto her stomach and let him do his job. Which was to slather lotion all over her.

Excuse me. She didn't even know this person and his big man hands were rubbing lotion all over her back? I couldn't watch. It was like watching them fool around. Brynn had no problem watching, sloshing her gum around. I half expected her to start eating a bag of popcorn.

I was the only one who was uncomfortable. On the other side of the pool, two women were wearing high-wedge heels, bikini bottoms, big, floppy hats, and chandelier earrings. And no tops. No tops, I swear! And yesterday, I jogged past a shoot on the beach and the model was changing into her bathing suit right there on the sand, just stripped down to nothing with people walking by and everything. In Cape Comet, Hillary High Beams was controversial just for not wearing a bra. But at least she had a shirt on.

After Jason left, Summer said, "I'll tell ya what, he had good hands. Allee, you don't know what you're missin'." She looked at the copy of *Sense and Sensibility* sitting on top of my bag. "You readin' that for school? Or you jest like it?"

"I just like it." I didn't tell her I'd read it five times. She was already making that you-are-so-strange-for-liking-to-read-school-books face I knew so well.

Brynn picked up my book and turned it over. "You have a boyfriend back in Rocket Land?" she asked.

Was she trying to have an actual conversation with me? Maybe she was. "I had one last year, but I haven't dated in a while," I answered. Lance and I were on cross-country together, but he'd broken up with me when the season ended. We didn't have much to talk about, so it was no big heartbreak when it ended.

"What about here?" Brynn asked. "Guys are everywhere."

I shrugged. "Why date anyone here when I'll be leaving in a few months?"

"So you read all those old romance books and you're about as romantic as a friggin' weather forecast. You don't even have a boyfriend. I don't get you."

I grabbed my book back. I didn't always get me either, but she didn't need to know that.

I turned away from her and asked Summer, "Did you have to read this for school?"

"I dropped out," Summer said. She was a high school dropout! I should have known. That's why she wasn't, well, too bright. I'd never known anyone who was a high school dropout. I wasn't sure what to say. I'm sorry? Sucks for you?

So I tried, "How do you feel about that?"

"Best damn day of my life. I went out and had a twenty-dollar party."

"What the hell's a twenty-dollar party?" Brynn asked.

Summer grinned. "You go to 7-Eleven and get a mess of Slim Jims and Funyuns, kick in a six-pack of beer, and then hit the drive-in."

"Jesus H. Christ," Brynn said. "I'm hungry." She spit out her gum with a *ftooie* and lit a cigarette. I couldn't believe they hadn't kicked us out of here yet. This was a fancy place.

Brynn's BlackBerry rang. She answered, "Hi, Ma. How was your party last night? Oh, yeah? Who was there?" Then she got up and drifted away toward the beach, with the phone to her ear. She talked to her mother like a best friend. I wished I had that with my mom. At least I had it with my sister now.

Only about ten minutes had gone by when Brynn hurried back. "I gotta go," she said, grabbing her bag. "Luca just called. He's picking me up. I gotta go, I gotta go." And she rushed off.

"I don't know what she's doin' with him," Summer said.

"I would never let a guy control me like that," I said.

Summer stared out at the sparkly pool and said, "Depends on the guy. Depends on what he can do for ya."

"Summer, that is so wrong." I started to talk to her about fem-

132

inism and what it means not to give up your power as a strong, independent woman. I tried to put it in terms a high school dropout would understand. I thought she was really interested, the way she was listening and not interrupting.

But then I realized she'd fallen asleep.

chapter 14

Dimitri told me that April the Great, Summer, and me were all on option for Uta Scholes. But I wasn't getting getting my hopes up. My options always got dropped, and the other two got booked on everything. Besides, Summer was sure she'd get it. I wished I was sure of at least one job. A month in Miami and not one. Dad's deadline was in a few days, and if I didn't book anything, he'd make me come home.

I couldn't face it. I couldn't even think about what I'd say to people when I went back to school, how I'd explain that this was all a stupid mistake. Who did I think I was, thinking I could model anyway? The worst of it was, if there was no modeling money, there was no Yale. My life was heading south faster than my bank account.

The agency taped me to see how I appeared on-screen. They wanted to see what I could improve to catch the eye of clients, promising they'd have more commercial castings coming in soon, more for my type. They said it had just been slow in my age range. I did get a callback on a regional Spanish-language commercial for Coke, and was put on option for a German catalog. They needed "teens mit enerchee" but I guess they decided I didn't have enough, because they dropped the option. Summer suggested I wear my ponytail higher next time so I'd look bouncy. I'd try harder to be upbeat next time. If there was a next time.

Because time was running out.

Something had to happen. Soon.

I went into the TV office and found Momma at her desk, talking quietly to a man in a chair next to her. He was wearing a wrinkled suit and white gym socks with dress shoes. There was something odd about him. Creepy odd. For one thing, he was doing all the talking. It was like he was talking *at* Momma, not *to* her. I couldn't hear what he was saying over the portable radio playing softly on Kate's desk.

Kate was on the verge of a nuclear meltdown, as usual. She was such a stress mess, she didn't even blink when she talked to you. It was really disturbing. "Allee, I'll tell you what I told your dad. We haven't had much in your age range for TV lately. But this week we're expecting two big ones, a Pepsi national and Cingular wireless."

I screwed up my courage and asked her, "Yes, but Brynn's shooting a Diesel jeans ad for Latin America today, so why wasn't I—"

"Diesel doesn't usually book girl-next-door types like you. Brynn's much, much sexier than you are, more fashiony. You two sort of have the same look, but you send off different messages on film. You're chalk and cheese in that way, you and Brynn." I understood what she meant. If the client needed wholesome pie, they saw Summer and me. If they needed the sultry, sexy girl, it was Brynn or Claudette. "Now, we looked at your tape, and Dimitri and Momma decided you shouldn't cut your hair, but you should wear it off your face more, so clients can actually see you. And you need to wear more makeup as well, blush and eyeliner. You look a bit faded on tape."

Did you know it is very nerve-racking when a person looks dead into your eyes and doesn't blink? "I know, it's just that uh, well, I haven't gotten—"

Beeeeep. A voice came through the phone: "Kate, you have a client on two." The man stopped talking to Momma and gave Kate a dirty look, like it was her fault her phone rang. He looked really angry. For a second I thought he was going to yell at her, but he just started talking to Momma again. He was making the hairs on the back of my neck stand up.

Kate pushed a button on her phone and talked into her headset. "Kate here. They confirmed April. Well, you only had second refusal on her—what do you want me to do, love, shoot her out me bum for you? Right, ring me back. Cheers." She held up the phone, brandishing it like a weapon. "That client better confirm

someone soon, or I'm going to beat myself unconscious with this."
Slam. "Now where were we?"

I didn't remember. I was distracted. The man was standing up now, grimacing at Momma. Did they have a security guard in this building? I glanced at Kate, thinking she must have realized by now that this man was dangerous, but she just looked at me, waiting for me to talk. "It's just that, uh, I moved here to make money for college and—"

He's reaching around to the back waistband of his pants!

I kept rambling, "Um, um, I was thinking you might have something, anything, just to show my dad that—"

He's pulling out a—

"OMIGOD!" I screamed. "HE'S GOT A GUN! CALL 911!"

"Allee—"

"CAN'T YOU SEE HE'S HOLDING A GUN TO HER HEAD? CALL 911! CALL 911!" I was at the door already.

"Allee, come back," Momma said calmly. "It's just part of Bob's monologue."

Monologue?

The man didn't look that scary or angry anymore. He looked kinda sheepish. He was holding the gun up. "It's a prop," he said. "A toy, actually." He opened his mouth, pointed it toward his throat, and pulled the trigger. Water squirted out.

Oh.

I went back and sat down. Just in case I wasn't feeling stupid enough, Kate knocked on my head and said, "Are you daft? Don't you recognize Bob from the Capital One commercial? He says, 'What's in your wallet' and all that?"

Ooooh, yeeeaaahh, *that's* who he was. I did recognize him now. He played the purse snatcher. "You're a really good actor," I told him.

"Thanks." He cleared his throat, put the gun back to Momma's head, and went back into his monologue.

Kate's eyes kept flicking to her computer screen. "What were you were saying, Allee?"

"Just that I'll do whatever it takes to work. I'll do anything and everything, I'll—"

"You see this gun?!" Bob suddenly screamed. "I'll kill you the way you killed my father, you whore!"

"Bob, could you keep it down?" Kate said. "Allee's trying to talk here."

"Sorry," Momma answered for Bob. "The conference room was taken. Allee, sweetheart, I'll be right with you. Keep going, Bob."

I started over with Kate. "I'll learn Spanish. I'll—"

"That's another thing, Allee," Kate said, butting in. "We're very cross with you about Saturday. Momma normally drops people who miss a booking, but since we had that conference call with your father, we're letting you slide. This time. And were you ever going to tell us that you don't speak Spanish?"

"I told Momma I didn't speak Spanish. What booking? What are you talking about?"

"I will blow your pretty brains out!" Bob yelled.

Kate slapped her hands over her Keira Knightley face. "Allee. Your comp says Allee Rosa with your stats in Spanish and you don't speak a bloody word of it. How do you think that makes us—and you—look? That movie would have been perfect for you."

Huh? "What movie?"

A vein was popping out on her neck. "You missed a direct booking. Do you understand? Not a casting. A booking. That sodding Argentinian crew that's filming at the Eden Roc. I tried getting you on Saturday, but your BlackBerry voice mail was full."

"It was my birthday. I stopped answering."

"Brilliant. Well, you were booked. I e-mailed the director a light box of fifteen models, and you got it. He booked you from your e-comp."

What? I was blown away by this earth-shattering news. I actually got booked on something! I didn't know anything about this. "It's not my fault," I said. "I didn't know."

Kate was pissed. "I called the apartment, but Summer didn't know where you were. That's when she broke the news that you're not bi-flipping-lingual." She threw her hands up and complained to some invisible person on the ceiling. "It was only a few lines. She could have faked it, right?"

Saturday. I was with Miguel, shopping. *Summer knew!* I'd even invited her to come with us. If Kate had known I was with Miguel, she could have called him on his cell and he would have given me the booking. *Summer deliberately screwed me out of a job.* When she knew I need one so badly.

Kate was waiting for an answer. "Right," I finally said. "I could have faked a few words in Spanish. And I'll do extra work, anything."

Beeep. "Kate, Dimitri on four."

"What do you want, Zorba? Yes, she's sitting right here. Pardon? Confirmed?" Kate's whole expression was brightening. The crease between her brows was softening. "Hold on one sec. Let me tell her."

She held the phone against her chest, blinked at me. "You're confirmed. You got it."

"What?"

"*Dietra* magazine. Uta Scholes just booked you for that big editorial, the Alice in Wonderland thing." Momma's jowly jaw was smiling. Bob with the gun was smiling. Kate was actually smiling. I was afraid to believe it. "Allee, love, you got it! Come give us a hug!"

I got the job. *I got the* Dietra *job!* I, me, myself, I got it! Feelings of relief and total joy flooded through me. "What about Summer?" I asked, still finding it hard to believe. "She was on option."

"They dropped her. April got booked too, with you, but you're Alice."

I beat out everyone, even Summer! Even April! Uta booked me! Finally. Finally! Yes!

Kate was back on the phone. "So give me the info, I'll tell her. Six-thirty weather check, call time is seven at the Raleigh. Clean hair, clean makeup. Bring chicken cutlets, nude stockings, strapless bra. Six-page spread, two full days at one fifty each." Only three hundred dollars. Editorials didn't pay like catalog because the tear sheets were sort of like your pay. *Allee, reality check: it would take you weeks to make three hundred at Wal-Mart.*

Hugs, hugs, hugs from everyone. And shouts of congratulations when I walked past the booking room, even from bookers I didn't know. Miguel rushed over to me and planted a loud kiss on my cheek, jabbering in Spanglish.

And then Momma, in her man-voice, the voice that I now loved, said, "Sweetie, this is going to give you a lot of exposure."

Who stole the tarts?

chapter 15

If my tutu and tights weren't a tip-off that this shoot involved a kinky Alice, the names said it all. There was Yaya (as in mocca-chocolata) the prop stylist; Havana (as in good time), the wardrobe stylist; Poe (as in Edgar Allan), the hair guy; Heini (as in tush), the makeup lady; Wolfgang (as in Amadeus), the art director; and Toto (as in not in Kansas anymore), Uta's shirtless assistant. Let's recap with Santa's new roll call, shall we? Yaya, Havana, Poe, Heini, Wolfgang, Uta, and Toto. Maybe all their parents were celebrities.

The "set" was a checkered picnic blanket set with English bone china and fancy finger foods. We were near a lake under some large oak trees, so it was nice and shady, but these trees had me a little nervous. Not because the light was tricky with the branches moving around making shadows, which is why Toto was anxiously checking the exposure every minute and muttering in Italian. The reason Yours Truly was worried was because of an allergy to oak tree pollen. Which means I'd be red-eyed and drippy-nosed if this shoot didn't get started soon. So far the prep was slower than a Norah Jones song.

Uta and Wolfgang were shuffling through photos, and Yaya was arranging fruit and tea sandwiches all around me while Poe touched up the gold paint streaks in my hair. "So, Allee," Wolfgang called, bending over the tripod to squint through Uta's camera. All I could see was the top of his head and the point of his devil beard. "What's your favorite magazine?"

"I don't have one. I've been reading tons of them lately and they all kinda look the same. I don't think any one of them really—"

"They all 'kinda look the same'?" Wolfgang squeaked in this super-offended tone. Poe and Yaya laughed nervously. Uta did too.

"She's hilarious," said Poe, sprinkling gold glitter on my head.

"So hilarious," agreed Yaya.

They were obviously not familiar with my "lighten up, Wednesday Addams" history.

Wolfgang pulled on his devil beard and huffed, "You know what? It is funny. The others do look the same. Not *Dietra*, of course, but the others." He and Uta started having another animated discussion in German. Poe whispered, "Allee, you were supposed to say *Dietra* is your favorite. Clients don't want to hear your real opinion."

"But he asked me for it," I whispered back. "He wanted to know what I think." Yaya and Poe giggled again at the very idea.

I sniffled. Louder than I meant to. My nose was getting stuffy.

Wolfgang called out, "Legs straight, Allee. Yaya, fluff out the tulle more." Yaya stuck her hands under my tutu and fluffed away.

"I found the Christian Louboutins!" It was Havana, the wardrobe stylist, who looked like she was probably a model when she was younger. "They were in the RV." She handed Yaya a pair of baby blue satin stilettos with long ribbons that exactly matched the ribbon woven through my gold-dusted hair. Yaya laced them up onto my feet, wrapping them around and around my ankles. Heini powdered me again and let me look in her hand mirror.

I was a glamour diva version of myself. This felt like an out-of-body experience, and yet it was my body. I had to admit, I *liked* the way this looked and felt. I liked the way this tight satin bodice squeezed me, the way the baby blue set off my skin tone, the way my legs muscles looked all sleek in these ankle-wrap heels. I had never, ever felt this sexy and grown up.

"Okay, do we have the kid?" Uta asked. "The kid" was a cute little preschooler in a white tuxedo and top hat, with an old-fashioned pocket watch on a chain. He walked up next to me and my heart stopped. The black hair, the brown eyes—he was a clone of Robby.

"You're not supposed to stare at people," he said, all quiver-lipped like he was about to cry. Havana walked up behind him and ran a lint roller up and down the back of his jacket. He didn't even turn around.

"I'm sorry. I didn't mean to. It's just, you look like my brother." He looked down at his shiny white dress shoes, lower lip curled out, eyes and nose starting to scrunch up. Oh, no. No crying, kid. There's no crying in modeling. "Are you the white rabbit?" I asked, trying to distract him. "Are you late for a very important date?"

He lifted his little head, saw Uta and Wolfgang pointing and smiling at him, saw his mom and Poe laughing, deep in conversation. They must have already known each other, probably from other bookings. Havana kept rolling her lint roller up and down, as if his back was a wall she was painting. All of them were blind to the fact that this kid was about to bawl, until he exploded into a full-blown wail. His mother scooped him up, knocking his top hat to the ground.

"Everybody's making fun of me," he sobbed, wrapping his legs around her waist.

"Don't wrinkle the suit!" Havana yelled.

Yaya smoothed out the blanket where the kid's mom had stepped on it while the mom calmed her son down. In the meantime, a dirty old van drove up and a man with a handlebar mustache and a tie-dyed T-shirt got out and walked over to us. He was holding two cages. "Hey, hon, where do you want these rabbits?" he asked Yaya, who glowered at him. He gave me a long, icky look. Then, in a voice as slimy as the filth under his fingernails, he went, "What do we have here? Alice all grown up? I'm into that, yessir. Or I'd like to be into that, heh heh heh."

Kill me now. Kill me immediately, if this letch was hanging around.

Unfortunately, he was, and I didn't have a knife to slit my throat. He was supposed to get the rabbits in case they went out of frame, but they were just sitting there. It occurred to me that they might be drugged. I wondered if I should report this skeez to PETA.

Uta was giving me directions. "Okay, Allee, you're just waking up, you see the boy, you look surprised, sweet and innocent, ya? Let's go." *Snap. Snap.* "Not so stiff, chin down, tilt your head a little. Soften your face, Allee, you look angry. Better." *Snap. Snap.*

Wolfgang was chiming in, "Relax your shoulders, that's it. Look at him, smile just a little bit, not too much."

The kid and I saw it at the same time, wet circles under Fluffy and Hoppy, spreading, larger and larger. By some miracle, our bunny buddies had decided to urinate in unison. I'd swear they planned it, like a protest. Call me immature, but it was really easy to smile now. For me and the kid. Nobody saw the pee yet but us, and it was our own private joke.

"Wow, that's it, you two are really connecting, now you've got it," said Uta. *Snap. Snap.* "Ya, look at each other, openmouthed smile, show surprise, both of you." She stood up. "Great, got my shot. But let's do a few Polaroids."

I felt a sneeze coming on. My nose was tingling, and so were my eyes. Uta stopped shooting. "Allee, is the sun bothering you? Close your eyes. Good, open on three. One, two, three. Open." *Snap.*

Except I could barely open them. I needed a tissue. "Ah . . . could I have a . . . a . . ."

"The blanket, the Hermès blanket!" shouted Yaya. "Those fur-balls are pissing on it!"

"Ah . . ."

"Don't sneeze on the tutu! It's a Gaultier!" Havana shrieked.

"Take the Kleenex!" Yaya urged, waving a tissue in my face.

"Ah . . ."

"Not on the dress! Not on the dress!"

"CHOO!!!"

Silence. Then two more sneezes. Silence again. Even the rabbits were holding their breath. Until they completely freaked, running away, scattering the china and sandwiches and fruit, sending the pervy animal handler in hot pursuit, and prompting a scream out of Poe that could have shattered his Dior Homme sunglasses.

"*Salute!*" Toto said to me. "Eet mean, eh, like-a gesundheit."

I checked my clothes. No signs of wet spots or damage. Only poor Yaya got the brunt of my sneezage, smack-dab in the middle of her face, but all she did was wipe it with tissue and say, "Those goddamned rodents ruined a nine-hundred-and-forty-dollar cashmere and wool Hermès blanket. How am I supposed to send this back to the PR house now?" That bit of info got Wolfgang and Uta's attention, and they started shouting in German. Nine hundred and forty dollars for a blanket? If the blanket was worth that much, how much were these clothes?

"What do you expect from rabbits?" Poe said. "The only thing they're good for is collars and cuffs."

"I like them with black olives and a pinch of salt," said Toto, kissing his fingers. "*Delizioso.*"

"How's the makeup?" Heini asked, examining my face like a doctor searching for a flesh-eating virus. She whipped out a Q-tip and a mascara from a pocket in her makeup belt. "Your eyes need a redo."

The kid was handling all this just great. He was standing stock-still with his finger up his nose, waiting to see what happened next. And that got me laughing. Big-time. Jumbo-size, two-ton buckets of whoop-ass hoots. The ridiculousness of this whole scene hit me, all of it. The rabbits, the pee, the blanket, the names, the kid, my outfit, the money. All for a picture. It was just so silly, really, when you thought about it.

Our second location was at the Versace mansion. It was easy. I just had to look into a mirror. On the way to our last location, our RV got stuck in late-afternoon traffic on the MacArthur Causeway Bridge, and Uta and Wolfgang started worrying we'd run out of time for the last shot, but I didn't mind the delay. The view was so choice you could eat it with a spoon: water on both sides of us, luxury cruise ships to the left, private boats to the right, puffy clouds and blue sky above it all.

Now we were at the Delano hotel and I was wandering around in my sundress, exploring. The crew was setting up outside, and we'd just done hair and makeup in one of the hotel rooms. Poe fixed my hair in two high pigtails like I wore when I was five, then put a big white bow in my hair. I guess they wanted me to go younger-looking for the next shot, like a more traditional Alice. I hoped so.

Models usually waited in the hotel room or the RV until the photographer called them, and I really should have been getting dressed for the shoot, but I wanted to walk around this beautiful hotel. The lobby was shaped like a huge tube, open at both ends, with a breeze blowing through it, white curtains where walls should be, giant furniture that didn't match, and titanic columns. The floor was so slick it was like walking on cherrywood diamonds. There was so much to take in. That wall had a harlequin pattern. A chair over there had high-heeled shoes for feet.

"What story does this all remind you of?" Uta asked me, coming out of the ladies' room.

"Story?" I scanned the kooky tall, overstuffed chairs, the Blue Door restaurant. It dawned on me that this whole breezy tube lobby might be designed to give the sensation of falling. Falling past crazy furniture and doors? *"Alice in Wonderland?"*

"Ya, that's right! Philippe Starck had it in mind when he redesigned this hotel." Uta swept her arms out. "All this inspired the idea for the shoot. It's a beautiful thing when art inspires art." Art? I wouldn't exactly call what she did art. She took pictures for catalogs and magazines. She created pictures that convinced people to buy criminally overpriced clothes. What was so artistic about that?

We went out the back doors, down the steps, and onto the manicured garden area that had a life-size chessboard. The crew was in a corner of the hedged-in garden, setting up the shot and prepping the other model I'd be working with. She was lying on her hip and elbow on top of a round gray table. Toto was blocking my view, so I couldn't see her face, but she was wearing an ankle-length green skirt that fit her bony frame like a tight sleeve. I just didn't understand why she was wearing a bikini top with it. I could see her whole rib cage. Whoever she was, she couldn't weigh more than a paper plate.

Toto moved, and now I could see who it was. I should have known. It was that over-freckled exoskeleton, April the Great. Her eyes were painted in Halloween green and yellow to match her eyes. Miguel was right. They weren't ordinary eyes. They were more yellow than green. When she moved her head, their color changed with the light, like a stained-glass window. There was a hookah pipe next to her. She was posing as the rude caterpillar. How perfect.

"How did you get booked?" she asked in this completely lifeless, bored way. She must have recognized me from the catalog casting. "You don't look like the editorial type."

I cocked my head like Brynn did, in the manner of one tough biatch. "Uta said she wasn't looking for editorial types. Like you," I added, like it was an insult. Although I knew that editorial, fashiony-looking girls were considered a lot more prestigious than commercial types like me.

"I get these magazine jobs all the time in New York and Paris."

"Well, we get them here sometimes, in between all the catalogs," Poe said, tucking in a loose strand of April's bun. "I'm sick of New York getting all the credit."

"I have to pee," April said, climbing off the table and shuffling away with baby steps because her skirt wouldn't let her take big ones. I saw why the skirt fit so tight. It was clipped with clothespins all along the back seam.

"You're not allowed to pee!" Havana yelled after her. "You're already dressed!"

Poe sighed dramatically. "The thing with caterpillars is, once they turn into butterflies, they still have the face of a bug."

"I think she looks like more of a praying mantis than a caterpillar," I said.

"You're terrible, I love you. But have you seen her on film? She's phenom." I hated to say it, but it was true. Miguel had showed me her book online. Her photos forced you to look at her, she was that good. In person, she was a dead fish, but her pictures practically screamed off the page. It was so mysterious; it bordered on sci-fi. "When I first saw her, I thought she was too special to work a lot. Imagine that."

"Too special?"

"'Special' is a term in the business for weird-looking, but in a good way, like Uma Thurman."

Havana grabbed me by the arm. "Where have you been? It's getting late, we're losing light. Do you have your chicken cutlets with you?" She pointed her thumb at Uta and Wolfgang, who were bent over some photos in an intense conversation. "They want mombo cleavage."

I nodded, rifling around in my bag. Where were they? Let's see here—agenda book, BlackBerry, stockings, two thongs, two strapless bras, clear nail polish, breath mints, *Jane Eyre, Alice in Wonderland, Rolling Stone,* Post-its, hand mirror, iPod, hair spray, Luna bars, Vaseline, SAVE DARFUR T-shirt, shorts, rubber bands, Q-tips, Visine, Tums, Excedrin extra strength, lotion, headband, gum, tissues, wallet, water, tweezers, razor, nail file, talcum powder, carrot oil, sunglasses, two bandannas, flip-flops, baby wipes, hair clips. Havana had her hands on her hips. "I know they're here, somewhere," I said nervously. They had to be. They were on my checklist. I started pulling everything out.

The bag was empty. They weren't there. Oh, no. Could they have fallen out? No. Someone took them out. Someone stole my chicken cutlets! I bet it was Brynn. "We really don't have time for this," Havana said, tapping her foot. *Think fast, Allee, think fast.* I showed her my gym socks. "Will these work?"

"That's cute. Very funny." She shouted to April the Great, who'd just gotten back, "Do you have chicken cutlets with you?" April said no. Havana looked ready to kill me.

My BlackBerry went off. Saved by the vibrate. "Hello?"

"Hey, girl." It was Claudette. "I'm at Go-Go. Thought I'd bring some takeout and treat you for dinner, since it's your first booking. What do you want?"

"Thanks, Claude. What I really need are chicken cutlets."

"In a salad?"

"No, in my bra. I need the other kind. Badly. It's an emergency."

"I got mine on me. You want to borrow?"

"How soon can you get here?"

Claudette appeared in two minutes, wearing a tube top as a skirt. It didn't quite cover the bottom of her butt cheeks. Mars was peeking out of her model bag. Some of the crew knew her. They were really busy, but they took a second to say hello. She bounced around hugging some of them, kissing on both cheeks. She even hugged Toto, who was all sweaty with no shirt on. I would have gagged, but Claudette didn't mind. Maybe that was why she seemed so sophisticated, because nothing fazed her. She seemed . . . open. To everyone and everything.

Yaya snatched the bag of takeout Claudette was holding. "No food near the props. This is going in the RV."

Havana was marching toward us. I chanted under my breath to Claudette, "Chicken cutlets chicken cutlets." She pulled two dark brown silicone inserts from her model bag.

Havana yelled, "Are you both blind?" and grabbed them. "Allee, you're white. And the top you'll be wearing is white. These'll show through. You'll look like a zebra."

"Um . . ." I said with my handy quick wit.

"I didn't know she was wearing white," Claudette said, taking them back, out of Havana's hands.

April craned her head to see the dark cutlets. Her thin lips were actually smiling. So were Poe's. Silent earthquakes of laughter shook his body. The whole crew thought it was hysterical. Even Toto was in on the joke. He rubbed his chest. "She gonna look-a like domino titties. *Qué idiota estúpida*, ha-ha-ha."

My face was hot. I'd never felt like a bigger dummy. How did I go from "Jane Brain" to "*idiota estúpida*" in a matter of weeks? This wasn't my fault. It wasn't Claudette's either. How dare they call us stupid? "I'm in gifted!" I wanted to yell at them. "I'm the smart kid!"

"Stop laughing at her," Uta commanded, and they all stopped. I knew Uta had that teacher quality from the minute I met her. "This girl is from a small village. It's her first booking." Exactly! Forget what I said about gifted. I was the village idiot, I knew nothing.

"She could have been more prepared," Havana whined. "We told her booker to make sure she had chicken cutlets. I'm calling her agency."

"No!" I shouted. The idea of Dimitri or Kate or Momma telling me off filled me with dread. Or worse, they'd laugh at me like everyone here was doing.

Havana threw her hands up. "Now the pieces won't look right. What am I supposed to do?"

"Use tape," Poe said, and then he did something that stopped my breath mid-lung. He grabbed my breasts and mashed them together! Excuse me! I was a person, not po-tatas. What was with the sudden grab-and-grope? I was stunned, too paralyzed to speak or slap him or anything.

He let go, and then Havana did the same thing! What was going on here? How dare they! Except I couldn't honestly say they were assaulting me. It was more like they just forgot their hands were touching a human, not a couple of Nerf balls. Havana lifted them, then let go and said, "Cutlets would be better, but yeah, my tape'll hold those." She looked me straight in the eye and said, in a voice that chilled me to the bone, "It'll leave a rash."

Havana and I went back to the hotel room, where I stripped down so she could tape me, and let's just say, if I thought she was feeling me up before, that was nothing.

Then she took out what I was supposed to wear.

It was underwear. Victoria's Secret type underwear. The really skimpy kind. The bra was white with black trim. And very thin. And lacy. At least the panties were black. That is, if you'd call two little black triangles held together at the top by a white ribbon panties. They were small. Really small. Like they could fit in a box of Tic Tacs. I'm talking small.

"Is there a problem?" Havana asked in a tone meaning there better not be a problem.

"Um, yeah. It's, well . . ." *There is no freaking way I'm letting them take pictures of me wearing this.*

"Look, Allee, this is La Perla. This set costs more than you're making."

"It's not that, it's just . . . I don't think I can wear this."

"Yeah, babygirl, you can," Claudette said, coming in. "Why so miserable, Allee? This isn't a wet T-shirt contest. It's not about sex. It's about fashion, you know, avant-garde."

"It's so easy for you. You're comfortable with this stuff."

"Allee, my father is a minister. When he found me in bed with a guy, he handed me a check, a Bible, and Mars, and then he told me to get out." A guy? I thought she was a lesbian.

"And did you?" Havana asked, looking totally intrigued.

"Yeah, I walked out of the house that day and moved in with my grandmother." Claudette shrugged. "Daddy and I still keep in touch. He sends me money sometimes, but my morals are nothing like his. I think it's moral to love yourself, love your body." She wagged her index finger at me. "There's more than one way to be a woman, and I'm doing it my way." Then she blew me a kiss, waved bye-bye, and strutted out, saying, "Have a good time with it. I would."

Havana was still holding up the lingerie for me to put on. "Maybe Uta could use Claudette for this shot," I joked, stalling.

"Let me give you some advice," Havana said. "You're not some moneymaker with a great track record, like April. You're a brand-new model who hasn't done squat. Now, if you ever want to get booked again on anything, cut the crap and get this on already. You've wasted enough time."

"The agency told me I didn't have to do anything I wasn't comfortable with."

"Oh, really? Wake-up call, you're a model. You do what the client tells you to do. If they tell you to pose naked, standing on your head with cheese sticks up your nose, you do it. I once did a job like that when I was a model."

"Really?"

"Yeah. The copy read, 'Do you know how to get your calcium properly?' Anything goes for editorial. Anyway, you've already accepted this booking. A booking, I might add, that every model and every agency was foaming at the mouth to land. Do you have any idea what these tear sheets will do for you? This is Uta Scholes. Be professional. Don't screw it up." She pursed her lips, held out the lingerie. "Now, you can call your agency and complain, but they saw the storyboards. They'll either yell at you or replace you. Or you can just do your job, which is to get this on and look pretty. Your choice."

It didn't sound like I had a choice. With dread, I let Havana help me get "dressed." Because of the tape, my cleavage hoisted up and exploded out of this bra, like two mushy rockets poised for takeoff. My shoes were like saddle oxfords, except they had four-inch spiky heels.

As Havana and I walked through the lobby, some doofuses in University of Miami baseball hats leered and took pictures with their cell phones. This was so humiliating. At least Havana was behind me, so the doofs couldn't see my butt, which, believe me, was hanging out in all its big school-bus glory.

When I got to the set, I stopped in my tracks. April the Great was wearing the same skirt and long earrings. But the bikini top was gone. She was leaning on her hand, with her other hand and arm covering the front of her small, bare breasts. Yaya was spraying her skin with something so it gleamed. The crew around her was doing their jobs. No one was leering or saying a word about it. She was chatting with them like this was perfectly normal. And it hit me that in this environment, it was. Bare breasts were just no big deal.

Kind of put a different spin on things.

Wolfgang saw me and said cheerfully, "Well, aren't you a tasty cornflake?"

Toto looked me up and down and said, "*Bellissima.* Everything look very good." But the way he said it didn't gross me out, not like the college boys had. He said it the way my dad told a waiter at Fuglies Barbeque that everything looked good when they brought out the ribs. It kinda lightened my mood, almost made me want to laugh. Almost. If I laughed, the tape might dislodge and then the rockets would take off.

I walked over to where April was, near the table. Her yellow-green eyes took in every inch of me, but she didn't say a word. Uta put her hand on my shoulder. "We're going to pose you lying in the grass, looking up at this caterpillar here." She smiled at April. "I want you to look something like frightened, you're not sure what is happening with this caterpillar, ya? Remember when I asked you to look scared at the casting?" I nodded. "That's the expression I want." She studied my face. "What's the matter?"

I'm not used to being practically naked in front of a bunch of people I've only known a few hours, and I think my nipples are showing through this bra, that's what's the matter. "Nothing's the matter. Really, I'm fine." I was determined to be professional, like Havana said.

"No one will see this in your village, if that's what you're worried about. *Dietra* has a European circulation."

"That's good, because people in my village don't take pictures like this."

She chuckled. "You look perfect, exactly the right mix of naive and sexy. It's a strong image, you showing skin. Like Alice shedding her innocence, you see."

I'd gotten so much advice lately. *You're booty-licious. Flaunt it. . . . Step out of your comfort zone. . . . Show your fabulosity. . . . Let yourself go freaky deaky. . . . Drop your inhibitions. Be brave. . . . Until you believe you're beautiful, you're not going*

to be comfortable with your body. . . . Be that beautiful girl in
your head. . . .

I could do this.

Uta offered me a water bottle with a straw in it. "Take a drink before we start. Use the straw so you don't ruin your lipstick." I hesitated. "Go on." Panic was rising in my chest. This could have been just like the drink that Alice in Wonderland took, the one with the sign that said DRINK ME.

After she drank it, she changed.

And so did I.

chapter 16

April was right. I wasn't a fashion type. *Dietra* was the only fashion editorial booking I ever did. But things started to happen after that shoot. It could have been Uta's layout that created a buzz around me, or the commercial castings that suddenly came around. It could have been that I wasn't weighed down with papers and tests and grades for the first time in my life. (I'd decided to take incompletes for my online classes. My teachers said I could finish them in the summer.) It could have been the acting workshop, or just plain luck.

I thought it was me. Something started to change in me after that *Dietra* job. I began to let go, let myself out of the heavy box I'd created my whole life, full of responsibilities and academic pressure. I started wearing my new clothes, putting on makeup more often. Some days I looked like a total girly-girl, the kind of girl I'd always ridiculed.

I was starting to look a lot like The Fluff. But I was feeling more and more like Alice.

March was turning out to be a busy month. I got booked on two small nonunion commercials, a spot for Pollo Tropical restaurants, and a small part in a local car dealership spot where I had to wave my keys from the driver's seat of a Ford Focus and shout, "Thanks, Dad!" I did a print job for a Mexican furniture company's online catalog for $350 where all I had to do was sit on a canopy bed in a nightgown and pretend to read.

Momma made me get a head shot and résumé, which led to Summer and me getting to be featured extras in a Mark Wahlberg movie. Now, before you ask if the glamour would never end, let me tell you, that job sucked. We stood for twelve hours on a hot sidewalk, and guess who the second assistant director yelled at? Yours Truly. First for looking directly at the camera and then for the bigger sin of looking directly at a principal actor. I couldn't help it. Mark was way, way shorter than I thought.

So I had a few commercials under my belt, and Momma said I might even book a Big One this season, a national. Things were looking up. Money was trickling in. Yale was really going to happen if things kept going in this direction.

It was eleven-fifteen. I could hear my roommates through the door.

Summer: "The Brazilian pills work. I ain't been hungry at all lately. Y'all want one?"

159

Brynn: "No, they make my heart race and give me head-aches."

Claudette: "That happened to me when I was juice fasting."

Brynn: "You don't even need those pills, Summer. You eat pizza every day and never gain a friggin' pound. I hate you."

It was the same mind-rotting hour of babble every night—fat grams, calories, carbs, diet tricks. Honestly, this industry really did hurt women. None of us ate right; Brynn ate practically nothing and used laxatives all the time. I was lucky because I was a commercial type and didn't have to look skeletal like Brynn, but I was always weighing myself now, like the others. Women shouldn't have to abuse their bodies for any job. But we did.

I was tuning out most of it, in the bathroom, door locked, staring at my reflection, trying to remember I'd never celebrated my birthday and I *should* have been going out; trying to remember I'd made a little money now and even though every penny should have gone to the Yale fund, I was long overdue to go out; trying, most of all, not to call myself a hypocrite, because it wasn't exactly a feminist staring back at me in the mirror.

It was Alice. Hell-o, Alice. "You are looking good tonight," I whispered to that girl in the mirror. Tight, short dress, no bra, high heels, curled hair, big hoop J.Lo earrings, glossed lips, false lashes. I hugged myself, whirling around to check out the backless part of me in this dress. It made me almost giddy. I loved it. It was beyond my control. And no one had told me it felt this good to look this hot. Never in my wildest dreams did I think I'd ever walk around without a bra like Hillary High Beams, but here I was, braless and whatever-no-big-deal about it.

The sound of a motorcycle roared, then chugged outside the

window. "Luca's here. Meet you guys there," Brynn said. I heard the door creaking open. "Your names are on the list. Don't forget your VIP passes. Doors open at eleven forty-five." *Slam.*

Tonight, I'd make her sorry she ever called me a buzzkill. I opened the bathroom door, walked out.

Claudette and Summer didn't speak. They just read me, starting with the vintage black stiletto pumps (classic Charles Jourdans circa 1983—a major find, according to Miguel) right up to the loose curls falling down my back. Claudette slowly walked a circle around me. "Allee, you look *mm-mm* good."

"You really think so?"

"Babygirl, you are fabulosity."

Summer still hadn't said anything. Why didn't she? I couldn't tell what she was thinking either. She just kept looking, chewing on her lip and shaking her head. "So, Summer, what do you think?" I was dying to know.

She crossed her arms, smiled a lopsided, icky smile that I hadn't seen before. It was so bizarre, it sent a shiver down my spine. "Reckon I been a horse's butt all this time. Jiminy crawfish, Allee. I didn't know ya had it in ya."

SoBe looked different in the dark. Forget the daytime gumball colors. Neon signs glowed in lime and fuchsia, strings of electric lights coiled around palm trees, even the sky was screaming for attention with a full moon tonight. And on the sidewalks, it was a look-at-me contest, a parade of toned bodies with bronzed skin, all traveling in packs, decked out in linen and satin and leather. I tried to pick out which of these rich-looking people were small-towners, pretenders, like me. Everyone and everything was competing for the spotlight, but as usual, it was Summer who stole it.

Not one person passing us could stop themselves from staring at her. Some even turned around to catch another glimpse. She didn't notice them. She was too busy complaining about how her starlicious talents were being wasted. "I'm a killer actress. I book almost every damn commercial she sends me on and she still don't push me for the big movie roles. Just 'featured extra' parts or bit parts with a couple lines. I didn't even get upgraded on that Mark Wahlberg movie."

"Same here," Claudette said. "And I'm a good actress too, as long as there's no dialogue in the script." She was serious. I kinda understood what she meant, though. I'd seen it at castings. Some models could show all kinds of emotion on film; blushing bride, happy shopper, thoughtful friend. But give them dialogue and suddenly everything goes flat. I'd seen it go the other way too. Models who were great with dialogue couldn't always show the right emotion if there weren't any words to help them. So far I'd only gotten booked on no-dialogue jobs.

"Momma won't send your reel out unless you do a monologue for her," I said, repeating what I heard Miguel tell another model once. Summer didn't say anything.

"Yeah, I heard that too," said Claudette. "Momma puts all talent into three categories: models, actors, and models who can do dialogue. That's why she makes you do a monologue, to see where you fall."

"Horseshit!" Summer fumed. "Niki Taylor, Janice Dickinson, Cameron Diaz, *and* Heidi Klum all modeled right here in Miami before they were famous, and I bet they didn't have to do no stupid-ass monologue." I'd never heard Summer t/ words around like that. She usually said "sugar an "cheese Louise" when she was mad. In fact, I'd never heard her complain before either. She was acting very un-Summer-ish.

Which got me thinking. She had apologized like crazy for not giving me the message about being booked in that Argentinian movie and I totally bought it at the time, probably because I was so excited about getting the *Dietra* job, but what did I really know about Summer? All I knew was that she was always "on," with good posture and a quick smile. Living with her was like having a puppy around. A puppy who could talk and show you things. But nobody was that helpful and nicey-nicey all the time. Maybe it had all been a front. A front that a "killer actress" could pull off.

"I'm fixin' to be as famous as them someday. More famous." She spun around to walk backward for a few steps so she could face us. "You jest wait." And she was off, stomping ahead of Claudette and me, her long legs taking her onto the next block in no time.

Maybe it was just a bad mood. I didn't think Summer could have a bad mood. Brynn was the one with the bad moods. "What was that all about?" I asked Claudette, who just shrugged. She was sporting her usual outfit of naked this evening, made up of two pieces of tied-on gauze. She was also holding Mars under her arm like a bizarre accessory. I could see right through that gauze and so could everyone else, which was just what she was going for, bouncing down the sidewalk like it was a runway. Although, to be fair, I'd been watching her for a while and she didn't give off a slutty impression, not really. She wasn't scamming on any guys. It was more like she was a free spirit, so happy with her body she wanted the whole world to see every inch of it. Hillary High Beams popped into my head. Maybe exhibitionism was only slutty in a small town?

"What's up?" Claudette asked me. "You look so serious."

"Nothing. Just thinking."

Claudette stepped behind me, and I just knew she was going for a touchy-feely. Sure enough, she rubbed my shoulders as we walked. "Allee, try not to think too much. Just have fun."

Just have fun, the South Beach motto. "I will. Don't worry." I'd change their opinion of me. They'd see. I was feeling the urge to break free and let go tonight.

"Thanks, Dad!" some guy called out to me as he passed, recognizing me from my Ford dealership spot. He waved his keys, like I did in the commercial. Then he told his friend, "Hey, that's the girl from that commercial." I flipped my hair and glanced back. They were still staring. Summer was usually the one who got recognized, especially since she'd done that Ludacris video.

I guess Summer wasn't the only one who could get attention.

I saw Brynn. She was a few yards ahead of us, behind a velvet rope in a silver, metallic strapless dress, smoking and blowing smoke rings. Luca Lizard-face was next to her, pacing and talking into a headset, near a tank of a guy with tree-trunk arms. The marquee above them read TONIGHT DJ LAZ, THE PIMP WITH THE LIMP, AND THE SEX-O-METRA DANCERS, A LOCO LUCA PRODUCTION. There was a crowd waiting to get in, spilling off the sidewalk and into the street. Limos and cabs were pulling up to the curb.

Brynn saw us. Her eyebrows lifted when she realized it was me under all this glammed-out gear. Then a slight tilt of her chin, a nod of approval. Satisfaction ran through my veins. Luca said something to tank guy, who lifted the rope and motioned for us to come to the front, cutting in front of the crowd.

I was going in.

The VIP lounge was upstairs, hanging over the dance floor like a huge balcony. It was dark, with tea light candles all over the bar, plush velvet couches, and glass cubes for tables. I didn't know what was so VIP about it. There was nothing very important happening, just a few people hanging out, talking and drinking, and two modely girls dancing. I was hanging over the rail, watching the action below. It looked way more fun down there with the bubbles and go-go dancers. The sight of women in cages did make me want to retch, but there were men in the cages too, so I guess it was sort of okay, like performance art.

I was drinking something sweet. Claudette had gotten it at the bar and handed it to me. It was in a martini glass and had chunks of pink Jolly Rancher candy all over the rim. The candy was delish, but the drink burned my throat unless I gulped it down fast.

That looked like Miguel down there, dancing. Yeah, and he was with Dimitri. I waved to them, spilling my drink. Claudette magically appeared next to me, holding out another one. "HERE YOU GO!" she screamed into my ear. We had to yell directly into each other's ear to be heard over the music. "BRYNN HOOKED US UP. IT'S ALL FREE TONIGHT." She clinked her glass with mine. "GUESS IT CAN'T HURT TO HAVE A BOYFRIEND IN THE PARTY BIZ."

"WHY DON'T YOU HAVE A BOYFRIEND?" I asked her.

"WHY DON'T YOU?"

My answer was to clink my glass with hers. I downed the last of my drink and started on the next one. It was getting hot in here. And I was smiling. A feeling of joy was welling up in me for no reason at all. "SO," I shouted, clinking my glass with hers again, just because I liked the sound of it. Then I did it again. I was going to ask her something . . . what was it? Gulp. Burn. Gulp.

Claudette was looking at me funny. She said, "SO . . ."

"WHAT?"

"WHAT WERE YOU GOING TO SAY?"

Oh, yeah. Now I remembered. "SO, ARE YOU, LIKE, A LESBIAN OR WHAT?"

"I CAN'T BELIEVE YOU JUST ASKED ME THAT!"

"ME EITHER!" Gulp. Burn. Gulp. "ARE YOU?"

"I DATE GUYS." She laughed. "AND GIRLS."

"OH." What else could I say to that? "GOOD TO KNOW." Gulp. Burn. Summer hadn't moved from her spot on one of the couches. She was in a heavy discussion with some dude who worked for a casting director. She knew he'd be here.

It was getting hotter in here. I loved the candy on this thing, this drink, this pink—

"Hey, biatch, this the one you were so worried about?" It was Luca Loco. He didn't need to shout. His voice was so deep, it was almost Darth Vader. His arm was hooked around Brynn's neck in a headlock. I bet he beat her. "This the one, biatch?"

"YEAH, BUT FORGET ABOUT IT," Brynn answered. "SHE'S NO COMPETITION FOR ME, ARE YOU, YALE? LAST MONTH YOU COULDN'T EVEN BOOK RESER-VATIONS, RIGHT? KIDDING, KIDDING. YOU KNOW I DON'T—"

"YEAH, YEAH, YOU DON'T FILTER," I yelled, cutting her

off. "I KNOW ALREADY." She blinked, surprised. Ha. I held up my empty glass. "UM, EXCUSE ME, ANOTHER DRINKOLA HERE?" Something about the way that came out made all of them laugh. I laughed too, but what was so funny? "IT WAS MY BIRTHDAY."

"WHAT, TODAY?" Brynn screamed.

"NO. LAST MONTH."

"WHY DIDN'T YOU SAY SOMETHING?"

"I FIGURED YOU'D BE OBNOXIOUS ABOUT IT." I never once thought about Brynn being obnoxious about it. But right now I felt like telling her she was obnoxious.

"Her? Obnoxious?" Loco said with affection, winking a hooded eye. "Never."

Brynn punched him in the arm. "SHUT UP, YOU FRIGGIN' MORON. GET THIS GIRL SOME CHAMPAGNE, FA CHRIS-SAKES."

I was drunk. And making out with a cute guy. He'd told me his name but it was so loud in here I couldn't hear him. These couches in the VIP lounge were pretty comfy. "GET A ROOM!" Miguel screamed at us, sitting down on the couch across from ours. Dimitri and Elmo-hair joined him. They'd all been dancing on the bar a minute ago.

I'd just gone into the bathroom and run into Elmo-hair in there (not sure if it was men's or women's—there were guys and girls in there and one transvestite wearing a nautical sailor dress who introduced herself as Mandy Lifeboats). Elmo-hair and I hugged like old friends. I didn't care that he hadn't booked me for that German catalog. I loved him right now. I even loved Brynn for popping open that champagne bottle. I also loved the taste of this Jolly Rancher drink.

April the Great had been in the bathroom too. I gave her a big hello even though she barely looked at me, like she didn't even know me. But I didn't care, because you know what? Drinking made me one friendly girl. Just ask The Cute Guy I Just Made Out With Even Though I Don't Know His Name. Now April was in the VIP room with us. She was dancing on the bar.

I pointed to her, leaned forward, and screamed to Miguel, "WE JUST DID A JOB TOGETHER AND SHE'S PRETENDING SHE DOESN'T KNOW ME."

He shrieked back, "TYPICAL. SHE'S SO MEET, GREET, DELETE."

Where was The Cute Guy I Just Made Out With Even Though I Don't Know His Name going? He'd just said something to me but I couldn't hear a word of it. He was gone. Now it was down to me, Miguel, Elmo-hair, and Dimitri. We decided to go to the Delano hotel pool bar for drinks. Well, they decided, but I was in. I didn't know where Claudette or Brynn had gone.

Brynn had yelled, "Hey, Allee, I'm going to the bathroom. You wanna come?" I was gonna go with her, but Miguel asked me to stay with him for some reason and pulled me away, and after a couple of Jolly Rancher drinks I lost them, right around when Prince showed up in the VIP room. Summer got her picture taken with him for *Ocean Drive* magazine. She was still sitting with him and his entourage on one of the couches when we left.

• • •

Inside the Delano, it was dim, with candles and curtains every-where. Tonight it was a fuzzy Wonderland, like I was dreaming this fashion show of pretty, shiny people in their pretty, shiny clothes: open necklines down to the belly button, sandals laced up to the knee, tattoos, body jewelry, short little dresses like mine. My wastoid eyes couldn't take it all in.

In the pool, two chairs and a table rose out of the shallow end. The life-size chess set was lit up on the grass. I swayed. The tiki torches were getting blurry.

"Allee, you okay?" Miguel asked.

I sank down onto an empty deck chair and curled up into a nice, cozy ball. Mmmm. Sleep.

"Get her an espresso," said Dimitri.

They sat me up and ordered one, plus a round of mojitos for themselves and nachos with salsa. I hogged the nachos, suddenly starving. They were really salty and good, but then I got queasy. Very queasy.

Uh-oh. I didn't feel so good. Elmo-hair's hair hurt my eyes. It looked like there were two of him. I blinked hard.

He'd just asked me a question. I wasn't listening. "What'd you say? And is my sweaty all forehead?"

"Ya, a little. I said, we would have put you on option, but we couldn't remember your name or your agency, and you didn't leave a comp card. We had nothing. What happened?"

"Ve had nussink," I parroted. "Vat hapnd?" I sounded so funny. Why wasn't he laughing too? He looked all pinchy-faced.

Miguel slapped my wrist. Hard. "Allee, you didn't leave your comp?"

169

"I gonna kill you!" Dimitri yelled.

Whoa. The room was spinning. There was a sour taste in my mouth.

Hold on. Focus. I might have been drunk, but I remembered handing my comp to the lady who took my Polaroid. "I left a comp."

"No, you didn't." But I was sure I did. Someone at Scarlett Print Productions must have lost it. I wanted to tell Elmo-hair, tell them all, but I was . . .

Nauseous now. Extremely.

Oooh, God.

Very sick now.

Very sick.

chapter 17

My tongue was growing algae. And I decided this bathroom floor was made of ice cubes, not tiles. But at least it was near the toilet. And at least I wasn't sweating or shaking as much as I was before, so the worst must have been over, the poison all gone now.

Nope. Nope, it wasn't. Here we go again.

"Christ on the cross," moaned Brynn when I was done. How long had she been standing there? "Sounds like you puked up a lung that time, Allee." She wet a washcloth and handed it to me.

I wiped my face. "What time is it?"

"Almost six. My call time's in a half hour." She said it quietly, trying not to wake Claudette. Summer hadn't come home last night. It wasn't the first time. When Brynn didn't come home, we knew she was with Luca, staying at a club all night, but when Summer didn't come home, she never told us where she slept. She was probably Prince's new drummer by now.

Brynn was in her version of pj's: sweatpants, socks, a sweatshirt with the hood up, eye mask on her forehead. She brushed her teeth, put in eyedrops. "You want crackers?" she asked, yawning. "I have some in my model bag. They help." I nodded, stunned to hear she owned food. She brought them to me and I took a mouse bite. My mouth was so dry the cracker felt like pencil shavings. But she was right. It helped.

I was about to get up for water when Brynn filled a paper cup from the faucet and gave it to me. "Why are you being so nice to me?"

"Why wouldn't I?"

"Because you don't like me."

"Who says I don't like you? Well, maybe I don't like you a little bit. But you're growing on me."

"I am?"

"Yeah, I gotta give it up. You weren't a complete pain in the ass last night."

"Thanks." My stomach rolled over with a loud gurgle. "Uch, I'm never drinking again. Never ever never ever again."

"You didn't pace yourself, you lightweight. I've done that." She leaned in to the mirror, inspecting her face. "You ever, uh, party with anything harder than drinks?"

"You mean, like drugs?"

"Yeah."

"No."

"You wanna try anything?" She tapped her nose. "I got some in my makeup kit, right here."

Holy shiitake mushrooms, she had cocaine in there!

"No, thank you."

I'd never been this close to a severely illegal drug before. This was serious. I had to get out of here. Now. Any second a police officer could barge in here and yell, "Freeze! Miami Vice!" and I'd wind up in the joint. Okay, not probable, but there was a one percent chance it could happen. Time to flee, vamoose, giddyup.

Except I stood up way too fast and was hit with a dizzy rush. I slid back down to the floor. So she did coke. That explained the sniffing and how jittery she got sometimes.

Her eyes met mine in the mirror. "Now that's ruining the nice little moment we're having here, see."

"What?"

"That look you're giving me."

"Sorry."

"I'm cutting back, just so's you know. I just need a couple lines for today. This client's making me jump on a trampoline, so I better rev up the engine." She put everything carefully away in her makeup bag, then pulled out a tube of Preparation H. This time I managed to stand all the way up. I definitely didn't want to be around for what she was going to do next. Crime was one thing, but bodily—oh, wait, she was only smearing it under her eyes.

Still, I couldn't leave. Too many questions. Like how often did she ski with Lady Snow? Was she an addict? Was I the only one who just says no? "Does Summer do it too?"

"What, this?" She held up the Preparation H. "Probably. It's the best for shrinking puffy eye bags."

"No. The, uh, the other thing."

"Oh. Nah, she doesn't smoke and she doesn't even drink much. Claudie used to do a bump now and then, but she stopped." Our eyes met in the mirror like they did before. "Listen, Allee, I don't have a problem. It's recreational, or if I need a boost for work, like now, or if I need to stay awake at night or not eat before a bathing suit casting. I take it as needed. Like a medicine. You get what I'm saying?"

"Yeah."

"You sure?"

"Yeah, just recreational, I get it."

"Good. So you don't have to be like that, all judgmental and crap. It's not like you didn't know. A smart chick like you, you musta picked up on it by now."

The smart chick had no idea. And it had been going on right under my nose. No pun intended.

Whoever it was better go away. It was bad enough that some idiot was knocking at the door on a Sunday morning. I was in Summer's bunk on top of her pink comforter with a magazine sticking to my face. I didn't have the strength to climb up to my own. O dear, sweet, loving Hangover Gods, make that knocking stop. I needed more sleep.

Good, Claudette was getting it. The door opened, letting in a shaft of light, or an ice pick stabbing my head, I wasn't sure which. Claudette answered it and said, "Allee, for you," and went back to her bunk. The door was open, but I couldn't see who it was. It better not be my parents. They were always asking when they could come down and visit. What if they decided to surprise me? I popped up jack-in-the-box style, banged my head on the top bunk, squinted toward the light, stumbled over shoes and clothes toward the door.

Whew. It was Lola, our next-door neighbor. She was a plus-size model who worked all the time. Today she was in her signature Salvation Army look—a patchwork skirt, woven top, and those Pocahontas moccasin lace-up boots that tree huggers wear when not in Birkenstocks. Anyone else would have looked homeless in those clothes, but pretty Lola could totally pull it off. Think larger-size Olsen twin.

"Allee, what happened to you? You look like the girl from *The Exorcist*. Or maybe *The Ring*." A distorted, alienlike image of myself in her sunglasses squinted back at me: scraggly, tangled hair; pale skin; dark circles; long, shapeless T-shirt; unexplained scrapes on my knees. "So, which is it? Were you, like, possessed by the devil, or did you just crawl out of a well?"

I couldn't even answer her. My head was pounding.

"Cool." She handed me a package. "Sorry, I forgot to give this to you. It got delivered to me by mistake."

"Thanks," I said, taking the package from her.

"Peace out." She went back to her apartment.

I opened it. It was a minidress, royal blue, stretchy, with an intricate crisscross of panels and tiny diamond-shaped cutouts all over it. The inside of the dress was emerald green. I thought it might be reversible. Under more tissue paper (by the way, tissue paper is really loud when you have a hangover), there was a skin-colored slip—I guess to show through the cutouts and give the illusion of nudity. It was incredible.

I read the card. *I made this for you. It's my design. It's reversible. And thanks for the necklace. The beads match my eyes. Love, Sabrina.*

The Fluff made this? And designed it herself? It looked like a top-designer dress from one of the high-end boutiques around here, not like a ninth grader from Cape Comet made it.

Someone had to have helped her. Except my mother didn't know how to sew. And Sabrina wouldn't write a lie on the card.

She made this, she really did.

Maybe I'd have to rethink calling her The Fluff.

Because some definite brain activity had gone into the making of this.

There was a group of guy models standing around in their underwear in the conference room. I could see them through the glass wall, all in identical tighty-whities. Miguel was Polaroiding them. Each one was more ripped than the next. I'd never seen so many six-pack abs in one room. Or tight buns. "Fruit of the Loom casting," said Tina, a men's booker, answering my curiosity.

Dimitri, hot as ever with a dark tan and scruffy face, was leaning out the back window yelling into his cell phone. "Do you hear this sound?!" He dropped a stack of some girl's comps into the alley. Some of them flew off into the wind. "That is the sound of your composite cards hitting the pavement, you *putana vlakas.*" Okay, I didn't know what a *putana vlakas* was, but it had to be bad. "You take a booking behind my back, direct, without going through me? This is how you repay me after everything I've done for you? Listen. Here goes your book." He dropped a portfolio out the window. A homeless lady put it into her shopping cart.

Miguel came out of the conference room and handed the camera to another booker. "Your turn." He kissed me hello. "Hoo-ee, I don't know about you, but I need some cold water. Did you see Frederico? That's a whole lotta man. And Tex? *Ay, mi madre*, everything really is bigger in Texas, you know what I'm saying?" I did see Tex. I knew what he was saying.

"Any castings for me?" I asked.

He sat down at his desk, chugged a bottle of water. "Let's pull up your chart." He started typing, concentrating on his computer screen.

Dimitri was still yelling into his cell. "When I found you, you were nobody. You were a sandwich girl at Subway. *Sto Diavolo!*"

"Sandwich artist," said Miguel, looking up at Dimitri. "They prefer to be called sandwich artists. I worked there in high school." Dimitri shot Miguel a murderous look. God, he was sexy.

Miguel touched the hem of my skirt. "Is that a Betsey?" he asked.

"Nope. A Catherine Malandrino. Got it at SoBe Thrifty."

"Ssshh, people will hear you. Don't be a bargain blabber. Except with me, of course. Hmph. Thought it was a Betsey."

Kate marched up to Miguel's desk. "Hey, Hobbit."

"May I help you?" Miguel asked sweetly.

"Did you put Allee on first option for Kohl's without checking with me first?"

"So what if I did?" Miguel said. "It's three days, a lot of money."

"My client wants her for the same days."

"It wasn't in the computer. Give your client a second option. We've got her first."

"She's commercial, on *our* board. You're supposed to check with our division first before accepting any options."

"Too bad."

"Come on, mate. Let me have her. "

He flicked his hand at her. "Dis-missed."

Her nostrils flared. "This would never happen at an agency in England."

"Buh-bye."

"That's the problem with you people. You have no manners!" She marched away.

"*We* have no manners?" Miguel called after her. "You people eat fish out of a newspaper!"

"Piss off!" she called back. "And don't ever put Allee on option for your bloody clients without checking with me or Momma first!"

Wow. They were fighting over me.

Brynn wanted to try on the dress that Sabrina had made me. Summer wanted to try it on. Claudette wanted to leave out the slip and try it on. I didn't let them. She'd made it just for me.

My thank-you note to her was pretty simple. *Thanks for the dress. You're a genius.*

Watching Momma and Kate on the phone was like watching a tennis match. I was waiting for Momma to get off the phone and give me my booking information. "They're looking for a Caucasian family of four," Momma's cigarette voice growled to whoever was on the phone. "Good-looking but not model types. Image Box Studio. For fifteen hundred."

"Pam, you *were* booked for a series regular, but they replaced you with someone younger," Kate explained into her headset.

"It's a cold reading," Momma said. "And talent are coming from Orlando. It'll probably be packed."

"Don't cry, love. I heard the story lines are so weak they're going to pull the plug on it anyway."

Momma hung up. "Allee. You're booked for Hershey's Kisses. Direct. It's print. You have to kiss."

"Kiss what?"

"Dunno," Kate said, hanging up. "A guy. Another agency booked him, so we don't know who he is."

"Some models don't do kissing, sweetie," Momma says. "Are you okay with it?"

"Um . . . he doesn't have a cold or anything, does he?"

Momma's laugh sounded like a hacking cough. "Not that I know of, sweetie," she said.

Hmmm. I hadn't been kissed in a long time. But I needed more info. Ever since the Uta Scholes editorial, I had asked more questions. We discussed my no-tongue policy for kissing strangers. A policy I'd just made up this second. I was hoping Momma hadn't heard about my little make-out session with that guy at the Delano. We discussed the rate, the photographer, and if I'd have to show any skin.

I wanted to know what I was getting into before I accepted a booking. I was a much wiser Alice now.

I was barefoot, standing on a rock at the most southern point of the beach, waves crashing and splashing my feet, the ocean churning behind me, my white linen dress blowing out behind me. It was all gooey-sweet and chick-flicky as I bent down, took Nando's face in my hands, we looked into each other's eyes, and I got ready to plant a kiss on his full lips. I made my face all wistful and romantic, the way I had practiced in the mirror earlier. And then I pressed my lips against his, and we went at it. He was Brazilian, and I didn't know what was going on in Brazil, but he sure knew what he was doing.

"No tongue!" Sean shouted. *Snap. Snap.* It was the same Sean who'd done my first test. When this ad came out, we'd be surrounded by floating Hershey's Kisses through the magic of computer animation. I was so confident now, more comfortable in front of the camera. I knew my angles, knew to be careful I didn't give too much chin when a photographer was shooting my face, knew how to stand so my body had the right line. And I believed I was beautiful. I told myself that before every job.

"That's a wrap!" Sean said, and he high-fived Nando and me. His Rasta assistant with the Jiffy Pop hat lowered the reflector, and the stylist helped me down off the rock. Some tourists were gathered on the sand, watching us. Two of them gave us a few claps, like golf applause. I took a little bow. Nando and I grinned at each other. It was better if he didn't smile. His teeth looked like Chiclets someone had stepped on. But the rest of him was hot.

"I can't wait till the ad comes out," I told him. He nodded, having, I'm sure, no idea what I'd just said. Who cared? He was the living definition of tall, dark, and handsome.

The sun was going down. Seagulls were swooping down to pick up crumbs in the sand. What a great shoot. I got to wear a gorgeous dress. And make out with a gorgeous guy. And make a nice little chunk of money. More and more, I really was Alice, living this wild fantasy.

My portfolio was missing. I'd looked all over the apartment, the agency, even retraced my steps back to the beach where I was watching Summer shoot for *Seventeen* magazine, but I couldn't find it anywhere. And I knew I'd had it this morning in my model bag, where I always kept it. I'd just had to go to two print castings looking like a jerk, because going without your book is like showing up barefoot for cross-country tryouts. Even though the clients had already seen my book online, on Finesse's Web site, it was still really unprofessional to show up without a portfolio. Dimitri would kill me if he found out. I had better find it.

Then yesterday I missed a TV casting for Clearasil because my alarm didn't go off and no one was here to wake me. Momma was so mad at me, she almost made me cry. She got me in at a later time slot, so I wound up getting put on tape, but one of the things she said was, "We finally get a casting that's perfect for you because they wanted great skin, and you have great skin, and then you don't even bother to show up? Allee, sweetie, I thought you were more responsible."

It was for a national too. Damn.

"Brynn took it," I told Sabrina on the phone. "I know she did. It's something she would do."

"How do you know for sure? I mean, even you can have a brain fart, Allee. Maybe you left it somewhere."

"Me? No. I am way too organized."

"What if you accuse this Brynn girl and then she goes ballistic? Like, what if you find it in your car or something?"

"I'd never leave it in my car. The humidity would ruin it. And how about my alarm clock? She must have unset it."

"You can't admit that you flaked for once. God, Allee. You are human, you know."

"I'm telling you, Brynn's out to get me. She's all pissy because of how I was 'all judgmental' about her using. And I never said anything to her about taking the chicken cutlets from my bag the day of the *Dietra* booking, too. I'm gonna search her stuff when she's out tonight."

"Just be careful."

Breaking news—Claudette's portfolio was full of nudes. In one shot, she was stretched out on a cliff with mountains and purple sky in the background, her arms curled above her head, at one with nature. Turn the page and her entire body was painted with reptile scales, and she was lying on her belly in tall grass. There were several tear sheets mixed in with shots of her where her bare body was draped across some guy's six-pack abs, or wearing nothing but blue skin cream, and even a girl–girl ad for some French perfume. Claudette's brown skin profiled against the chalk-white girl was like visual electricity.

I wanted to say she was exploiting herself with these naked pictures, but they weren't really offensive or disgusting, not like the porn magazines Jake and Scott had brought to school once. These shots reminded me of my art textbook. They glorified the female body, the same way artists had glorified it since the beginning of time, with artistic imagery. One photo was a version of Botticelli's *Birth of Venus*, with Claudette rising out of a shell.

So her ticket must have been her sex appeal, or sensuality or whatever, but more than that, it was her attitude. She was all about freedom, and it showed in every picture of her long body. I glanced up at her sitting next to me on the futon, engrossed in her paperback of Edith Wharton's *The Age of Innocence*. It was nice to have another reader in the apartment. Claudette and the countess in that story were a lot alike, now that I thought about it. They both kinda pushed boundaries of what was socially accept-able. Claudette was so into the story she didn't even notice I was going through her book.

"Hey, y'all," Summer said, coming through the door in her workout clothes. Her smile was fully charged. If modeling didn't work out for Summer, she could get a job at Disney World on one of those parade floats, smiling and waving to crowds.

She kicked off her sneakers, sat on her magazine-covered bed, and started sewing up a hole in a pair of tights. Another one of her cheap habits. Never mind that she was planning to wear those tights with a pair of Sergio Rossi boots she'd bought in Bal Har-bour at the half-off, bargain price of five hundred dollars. Hel-*lo*, Summer, you could buy a kajillion pairs of tights.

"Why didn't you ever go back to college?" I asked Claudette. "Why model? You're smart, you love literature. Is it the money?"

She closed her book, drew her knees under her chin. "No, it's not the money. I'm not even making that much yet, or I wouldn't be living here with you guys. I haven't worked in over two weeks."

"So why then?"

"I love to read, but I also love how beautiful I feel when I'm posing. I love seeing myself in pictures. I love doing the runway shows in Milan every summer, traveling to Paris, Athens, all over. But mostly, and this is the main reason, I love being able to express myself any way I want. This life's an adventure and I'm all for living it. By my rules." She sounded almost angry. I figured she was thinking about her father. He probably didn't think much of her naked adventure. She'd only talked to me about him that one time, at the Uta Scholes shoot, and never again. And she never talked about the rest of her family. I didn't even know if she had any. Summer was like that too. Not like Brynn, who was always talking about her "Ma."

Claudette went back to her book. Brynn's portfolio was on the coffee table. Time to look for her ticket. Her book was so her. It wasn't packed with smiley bathing suit pictures like Summer's or sexy artistic shots like Claudette's. Brynn was rock climbing in a black cat suit à la Lara Croft. She was a boxer, seminude and glistening with sweat. She was riding a motorcycle, waterskiing. Kissing a guy under an umbrella with ferocious intensity. The only one that rubbed me wrong was the picture of her sitting on her knees, topless, looking up at a man in a business suit.

"Hey, who said you could look at my book?" Brynn asked, walking out of her room. I knew she'd been late to a job this morning. Dimitri had left a furious message telling her to get her act together.

I closed her book. "Sorry."

She'd been snorting. I knew the signs now, the sniffing, the swiping at her nose, the jerky movements and blinking. And her mega-bitch mood. I never knew what to expect from her. Some days she was completely nasty and looking for a fight, other days she was almost semi-nice. "No, no, g'head," she said, crossing her arms. "Tell me. Now that you've looked at it, what do you think?"

"I love your whole book, except for this last one."

"Why?"

"The way he's looking down at you on the floor. It's like 'good little doggy' with that look on his face."

"That's his problem. What about my face?" *Sniff. Sniff.* "Huh? What about my face?"

"Your face looks great," said Summer.

"Yeah, you look amazing," I agreed. "But that's not the point. Images like these marginalize women."

"What'd she say?" Brynn asked, blinking at Summer.

"Somethin' 'bout margarine," Summer answered.

"She means," said Claudette, looking up from her book, "that the picture degrades all women."

"Whatever," said Summer. "See, Allee, you're not the only one what knows a thing or two."

"Great, now we got two of them." Brynn jutted her chin toward me. "One know-it-all living here is enough."

"I'm not a know-it-all," I said.

"That's not what Summer says about you," Claudette said, tossing her book aside.

Summer's blue eyes turned icy. She aimed them at Claudette, but Claudette turned her head and lit up a cigarette.

"Yeah, you do," Brynn said to Summer. "You say that about Allee all the time. You're full of it, Summer."

Summer talked about me behind my back?

"Thanks a lot, y'all," Summer said, throwing down her tights.

She was. She was talking about me behind my back, calling

me a know-it-all. My stomach tightened. "Summer?" I asked. "Did you call me a know-it-all?"

"Sorry, Allee, it just pops out sometimes." What else did she say about me? "I don't mean nothin' by it. You're as sweet as a speckled pup, it's just . . ."

"What?" I wanted to know.

"Well, you can git a little uppity, Allee."

"Uppity?"

"About how smart you are and all, you do get uppity."

"Yeah, you kinda do, Allee," Claudette said. "Sometimes."

Had they all been thinking that about me? That I was some kind of snob? That was so unfair. I was nice to everybody.

"Yeah, you are an uppity little brat," Brynn sneered at me. "Who the hell do you think you are anyway, saying I degrade all women?"

"I didn't say you degrade all women, I said the picture—"

Brynn grabbed Claudette's portfolio off the floor and chucked it. *Crash.* It knocked a framed print off the wall, one of the Mediterranean islands. The glass was cracked. None of us made a move to pick it up. I think we were all in shock, including Brynn.

The phone rang. "Nobody get that!" Brynn yelled. She picked up the phone, went into her room, said, "Hi, Ma," and closed the door.

"She's high," Claudette said quietly, carefully picking up the glass. I got up to help her. "She does a bump every day. Luca gets it for her."

"Best thing to do is steer clear," Summer whispered, looking toward Brynn's door.

I took a plastic garbage bag from the kitchen and helped

Claudette put the glass shards inside. "But she needs help," I whispered. "Shouldn't we tell Momma or something?"

"I reckon she knows," Summer said. "Brynn ain't the first model to use drugs. But y'all don't need to be gettin' involved. You can't help someone that don't want it."

chapter 18

I spoke slowly and watched my voice quality. "Allee Rosen. Finesse." I showed my hands, front and back, turned to the right, to the left, all the way around to face the wall so the camera could shoot the back of me, then forward again. My feet stayed on the mark, which was a line of tape on the floor. A guy named Blake was paired with me for this callback.

"Okay, action," the lady casting director said from behind the camera.

Our eyes darted everywhere, searching. I made sure the camera saw three-quarters of my face at all times. Just like we rehearsed in the hallway, Blake took me by the hand and led me to a stool with two soda cans. Only we had to pretend that the drinks were growing out of a bush.

"Okay . . . now you see them," said the casting director.

My eyes popped at the sight of these miraculous soda cans. I looked incredulously at Blake, then did the openmouthed smile of ecstatic joy while saying in my mind what I wanted my face to show: *Wowee-Kazowee! Look at these drinks growing out of a bush! This is fantastic!* Blake was trying to do the same, but he was nervous.

"'Kay, Blake, now pick one up and drink, come alive. Remember, this is for Taboo, an energy drink." Blake drank, trying to look like it was the best thing he'd ever tasted.

I was supposed to be a wholesome college-age kid for this, which was why I'd worn the high ponytail Claudette had suggested with the tight polo and plaid mini that Miguel had picked out. The client wanted good-looking "real people" types, not over-the-top gorgeous model types. I did the cheesy commercial laugh clients all loved. It came more easily now.

"Cut. You guys wanna do this part one more time? Let's do it again, 'kay?"

Blake put the can back and asked her, "What's my motivation?"

"Hah?"

"My motivation. Like, for acting. Why do I want to drink Taboo so badly?"

"You're thirsty. Why don't you go with that and see what happens. Do you need a motivation too, Allee?"

"No. I want to book this commercial. That's my motivation."

"Okay," she said. "Now the jungle has turned into a house party. Blake, you just stand there. Allee, you drink. Ready? Action." *Mmmm. Delicious.* I closed my eyes and sipped, transported by the flavor of carbonated water, high-fructose corn syrup, and psychotic amounts of caffeine. I'd tried Taboo before. It was like drinking a liquid hand grenade. *Yummy!*

"Okay, Allee, this is where you dance. Let me explain how the client wants you to—"

"We have to dance?" I interrupted. I thought Momma might have said something about dancing when she gave me the casting over the phone, but I was distracted. *America's Next Top Model* had been on and I was taking notes.

"Just you. Not him."

"But I've never danced in front of people. Not really, not in public," I said with panic in my voice.

"Didn't I see you grinding on the bar at Privé?" Blake asked.

"Must have been Brynn. People mix us up."

The casting director was looking at me funny. "You've never danced in public? Not even at a wedding or anything?"

"No. I've never been to a wedding."

"Never been to a wedding," she muttered. She cocked her head to one side. "So you're saying you *can't* dance?"

I bit my lip. "I'm not sure."

"Let me guess," Blake said, grinning. "You're an undercover freak. You dance alone. In the shower, in your bedroom . . ."

He had me. "Yeah, kinda."

"Well, let's go ahead and put you on tape, anyway," the casting director said. "Blake, you're done. You can go, thank you." Blake left and wished me luck. I'd need it. Because I was probably about to make a giant ass of myself. "Put some music on," the casting director called to someone I couldn't see in the room with all the equipment. No music came on. "Be right back." She walked out.

How was I going to dance on-camera? It had always been like a private thing. I didn't know if I could let go the way I did when I was alone, all uninhibited and loose and everything. But I'd also never thought I could pose all sexified in tiny lace lingerie in broad daylight either. If I could do that, I could do this. I wondered how Summer had danced. Her time slot was a half hour ago.

I closed my eyes and focused on what I'd learned in my workshop. I had to breathe deeply, rid myself of self-consciousness, let go, let flow, let insides show. Okay, I was feeling more relaxed. I pictured my room at home in my mind, my mirrored closet doors, all the moves I knew. I rehearsed in my mind.

The casting director was back. "Okay, Allee. When I hit the music, go ahead and dance, but stay on your mark. Smile, energy, have a good time, got it?"

"Got it."

She went back behind the camera. "And . . . action."

The music came on. It was Will Smith's "Welcome to Miami." Perfect. I closed my eyes and tried to get jiggy. She said energy, so I threw my hands in the air like I just didn't care. I shook it like a Polaroid picture. Or tried to.

I felt like a total fool. All my self-consciousness was back. I tried some hip-hop moves like Fergie did in her videos, but I had a feeling I wasn't pulling it off.

Uh-oh. Was I on the beat?

The music stopped. Well, that was a disaster. I opened my

eyes. She was smiling from ear to ear. "Perfect. Great job." That was unexpected. I thought I'd sucked.

Hmmm. Maybe I was better than I thought.

Nobody was home. I was in Brynn's room. I looked in her drawers, under the piles of clothes on the floor, all over her closet, in her suitcase. The last place I looked was under the bed.

And that's when I felt it. She pulled my hair. I hadn't even heard her come in. The pain was blinding. "Ow!" I screamed, grabbing my head. "Owowow, let go!"

She did. "What are you doing, going through my stuff?"

"Looking for my book." My head was throbbing. I wanted to cry. But no way was I gonna give her that satisfaction.

"I didn't take your friggin' book. Now get outta my room."

She didn't have to tell me twice. The door slammed behind me. Then I heard her throwing things and cursing. I had to get out of here. As fast as I could, I threw on my sports bra and running sneakers. I had one foot out the door when I heard a sniff coming from Brynn's room.

That wasn't what stopped me. I'd heard her sniffing in there lots of times. What stopped me was that it was a different kind of sniff. It was the kind of sniff that came with a sob. Brynn was crying.

I couldn't picture it. Crying was so . . . weak, so not Brynn.

I was torn. I had such an urge to get the hell away from her. I mean, she'd just attacked me. My head still hurt. But hearing her cry did something to me. I knocked on her door.

"Screw off!" she sobbed. I opened it anyway. Brynn was crumpled on the floor, hugging her knees and rocking, crying softly into a tissue. She looked like a little kid, a scared little kid. Nothing like the tough Brynn I knew.

It weirded me out, completely.

If I tried to comfort her, would she pull my hair again? Throw something at me? I couldn't just keep standing there, watching her cry. So, even though it was awkward, I got down on the floor and kinda half-hugged her, until she stopped crying. She smelled terrible, like cigarettes, sweat, and bad breath. I asked her what was wrong, but she didn't tell me. She just said, "Nothing." Her gravelly voice, usually so loud and strong, was shaky and small. "I'm okay."

She was so not okay. In fact, she kinda grossed me out, to tell you the truth. I still wanted to haul butt outta there, believe me, but at the same time, I felt sorry for her, I really did.

Because she was messed up and she knew it.

Summer and I walked into the agency at the same time as Monique. She was looking a little Harajuku Girl today with her para-Asian features and a pink headband over black blunt bangs, but also a little bit Austin Powers in a pink pantsuit and ruffled blouse. "Allee! Summer!" she cried, and earnestly tried to stretch her swollen balloon lips into a smile. She took off her sunglasses to get a better look at us. And I let out a yelp. She must have been in a fire. Her eyes did that half-sleepy, half-disgusted Garfield thing. "It's from a chemical peel. Bad reaction."

"Oh," I said.

"You always look beautiful," Summer said all convincingly. She really was a good actress.

"You'll know about peels someday," Monique said, and

pointed at some models lounging on the mint green couches. "You all will." They cringed, terrified. She turned to Bonnie, the receptionist. "Get me an appointment with Anushka. And tell her that bleach she used on my arm hairs last time gave me a rash." She turned back to Summer and me. "Make sure you check in with Momma. She's got good news for both of you." We watched her do a runway walk to her office.

"Girls, girls, girls," Momma said when we walked in.

Kate was talking into her headset. "Three hundred quid for head shots and the photographer didn't tell you to trim your nose hairs? You look like you're wearing bloody nose-hair extensions. You've gone off your rails if you think we can use these pictures. They're rubbish."

"Hey, Momma," Summer said, kissing her. "What's the good news?"

"You're both on first refusal for that national, the Taboo energy drink!" Momma said.

"That's great!" I shouted.

"Both of us?" Summer asked, brightening. "Well, butter my ass and call me a biscuit, Allee. We're up against each other again."

She might as well have said, "Start your engines." I felt my competitive juices flowing. "We sure are," I said, gritting my teeth in a grin.

"Can't you wax all that hair out?" Kate asked. "Bollocks, it hurts. So what if it hurts? Use a buzzer, then."

"I just put all the info on your charts," Momma said. "Summer, Otto catalog wants you on the same day, but I told Dimitri just to give them a second option, because this is for a lot more money."

"Thanks, thank you so much for sending me on that casting," Summer said, hugging Momma. "You're the best agent in the world," she gushed. She was such a suck-up to the agents. She was always bringing them little gifts and thanking them for every casting, every job. Then the minute she left the agency, she complained they didn't do enough for her. She blew Momma a kiss. "I gotta check in with Dimitri. Fingers crossed! Love ya!"

"I better check in with him too," I told Momma. "Thanks, you guys."

"Wait, Allee, we have to talk to you," Kate said, taking off her headset.

"It's about Brynn," Momma said. "Sit down." I sat. "She was supposed to be on location at six today for a sunrise shot. She was late a half hour, the sun had risen, and the client had a stroke over it. He wouldn't sign her voucher and he won't pay the cancellation fee."

"That sounds bad."

"That's not the half of it. Then her boyfriend showed up and they got into a nasty fight in front of the client."

"The crew said she reeked of alcohol and her hair was dirty," said Kate. "This is the second job she's been late to, and she's missed castings."

I kept quiet. I'd seen Brynn go to bookings drunk, but she managed to pull through and get the job done. Besides, what did they want from me? I wasn't the girl's mother.

Momma continued, "I've already talked to her, put her on probation, but I don't think it took. You know how much I care about all my girls. I love Brynn. Kate and I think she's got potential to be a big moneymaker. Dimitri does too. But she better stop partying so much and get off the drugs or she's done. I've seen it happen a thousand times."

"What does all this have to do with me?" I wanted to know.

"We'd like you to talk to her," Kate said. "We've already tried. We think she'll listen to you."

"She won't listen to me. She doesn't listen to anybody."

"You're very together," Momma said. "And you're almost the same age. You're a good example for her. You're booking jobs now, you're smart, you've got goals with your plans for Yale and everything. You could help her see how much she's hurting herself and her career."

"I don't know. I mean, why would she take advice from me? She's the experienced one. Maybe Summer could—"

"Just talk to her. Try, mm-kay?"

I nodded. Excuse me. How in hell was I supposed to talk to Brynn about anything? She wouldn't even tell me why she was crying. They were mental if they thought she'd listen to me.

"Thanks," Momma said as I walked out.

I was walking on Miguel's back in the corner of the booking room, watching a model leaving the accounting office with an envelope and a big smile. I happened to know she worked a lot. She was wearing wrinkled sweats, a T-shirt with a hole in it, and a faded baseball cap. There were splotches of dried zit cream all over her chin. If you thought models walked around looking perfect all the time, then you thought wrong. In fact, sometimes the ones who worked the most looked as sloppy as unmade beds when they weren't working, because when a day off came along without stylists and hair and makeup people working on them, they just wanted to sleep late, roll out of bed, and run around with no fuss, no muss. I'd seen girls at the agency in pajama pants and slippers.

What I didn't get was how this girl worked all the time. She was shorter than me and didn't even have good skin. "Now how does she do so well?" I asked Miguel. "She's always booked."

"Easy. She's a ready Betty."

"A what?"

"A minuteman model. That's her ticket. Always ready to replace a girl if there's an emergency or a last-second cancellation, like when April had that allergic reaction and her face blew up an hour before the booking. That girl was there in two minutes to take her place."

"Wouldn't they reschedule?"

"Not always. Sometimes they can't. That girl is great when you need her there in a pinch, or when it's off-season and all we have are nothing jobs. Clients love her and she'll do anything. Naked? No problem. A *mierda* rate? *No problema.* She's a *puta* and we love her."

"What's my ticket?"

"I'm still figuring it out."

Beep. Momma's cigarette voice came through Miguel's speakerphone. "Allee, you there?"

"Yeah, she's here," Miguel yelled from the floor.

I stepped down off his back. "What's up, Momma?" I called.

"You booked the national for Taboo! The client loved your dancing."

"Cha-chingalingaling!" Miguel sang, jumping up to hug me.

• • •

"Guess you'll be even more uppity now," Summer said to me when I got home.

"Hey, Summer, lose the attitude," says Brynn, trying on the new strappy sandals she'd just bought. She was in a good mood today. "Give the kid a break. She got the national, you didn't, stop being such a friggin' baby. Congrats, Allee."

"Thank you." I turned to Summer. "I wish we could both do the job." It was the kind of thing you were supposed to say.

Summer pulled out a suitcase from under her bunk and started throwing clothes inside. "It don't matter. I'm gonna be so famous someday, a little uppity bitch like you won't make no difference."

Stung, I backed away from her. I knew she wanted to book it, probably just as much as I did, but what was her problem? Did she turn on anyone who took a job she wanted? I mean, she wanted the Uta Scholes editorial and when I got that she didn't—

Wait.

Omigod.

Something went *ping* in my brain.

A realization was unfolding inside me. It was knocking around in my head, my stomach, my chest.

I knew what she had done.

"You took my book, didn't you?" I asked her. She stopped packing, unzipped her gym bag, pulled my portfolio out, and threw it at me. Claudette and Brynn looked like they'd turned to stone. "Why?" I asked. "Why would you do that to me? Someone as successful as you."

"'Cause there's always a new girl. Before you there was Issa, and I didn't let her get in my way either. Maybe the Uta Scholes job was just a fluke, like you said, so I didn't give it no nevermind. But soon as you came out lookin' like you did that night you came out with us, I knew. I didn't think you was no match for me till that night. Now this national. Momma's pushing you more than she's pushing me. There's tons of competition at castings. I don't need it from my own agency."

Brynn said, "Geez, I used to think Allee was a threat too, but steal her book? That's low, man."

"Just crabs in a basket, that's all. Gotta pull one down to stay on top." Summer smiled that bizarre, icky smile and pulled out a stack of composites from her gym bag. She chucked them at me. They were mine. "If you can't play with big dawgs, git off the porch."

I picked one off the floor. "Why do you have all these comps of mine?"

"I took 'em after print castings, if I could get to 'em. Pulled 'em right off bulletin boards, desks, right outta the client's pile. And I didn't even think you was a threat then. I just wasn't takin' no chances."

Claudette gasped. "You did not."

"She did," I said. That knocking feeling was going away. I was dead calm, watching the past few weeks flash by in my mind. "And you messed with my alarm clock. And you took my chicken cutlets. I bet you even tore down the sign at that German catalog casting so I wouldn't find the Polaroid room."

"All that studyin' made you real smart, Allee."

I was so angry, I could have hit her. "All that 'I'm just as sweet as molasses.' It was all an act."

"I act"—she picked up her suitcase—"because I'm an actress."

A red Mercedes convertible pulled up in front of the window. A man was driving, a midlife crisis type with a gray ponytail, at least fifty years old. Summer was eighteen. "I'm leavin' Finesse and I'm leavin' y'all. I was plannin' on leavin' next week. Been makin' so much money, I don't even know why I stayed so long."

She started to walk out, then dropped the suitcase and whirled around to face me. "You know what, Allee? Some of us didn't just go to the mall one day and fall into modeling. Some of us worked hard to get here. Some of us want this real bad."

"I know that."

"No, you don't. You act like this all don't mean nothin', like it's below you 'cause you're too smart for modeling, too high-and-mighty for all of us."

"I don't—"

"You do. But you jest wait. I'm gonna be so famous, so fierce, *Entertainment Tonight* will be calling you up for interviews just 'cause you lived with me. That's how come I was so nice to you, so you'd tell them reporters I was real helpful on the way up."

"Man," Brynn said. "You're a friggin' wack job."

"Delusional," I whispered.

"Y'all can make fun now. Someday I'll be a household name."

"What name is that?" I asked. "Darlene Mole?"

Hearing her real name threw her. Her eyes blazed. "You know why they changed your Jew last name, don'tcha?"

"What?"

"For the European clients. They don't like bookin' Jews." I

froze, completely paralyzed. A creeping sensation spread across my skin, like I was covered with a million ants. "Ain't smart enough to figure that one out, are ya, Yale? Too busy correctin' me like I'm a dumbass. Well, there's all kinds of smart and there's all kinds of stupid. Guess which one you are." She picked up her suitcase. "I'll be back tomorrow to get the rest of my stuff."

She slammed the door. We watched her get into the car and drive off. I sank onto the futon, limp and numb, and put my head in my hands. My hands were shaking. Claudette put her arms around me. Her shoulder was warm and soft. "That's not true," I said. "About my name, is it?"

"No," said Claudette. "There's Blaine Cohen on the fashion men's board. And Monique wouldn't do that. Neither would Momma or Dimitri or any of them." She gave my hand a squeeze.

"I never knew you had a set, Allee," Brynn said, rubbing her nose. "You got balls. What a psycho." Imagine *Brynn* telling me *I'm* the one who had balls. But I guess I did. Maybe my assertiveness problem was officially cured. She stepped toward me and I thought she was going to hug me, maybe the way I'd hugged her that day she was crying, but then she thought better of it and gave me a light punch in the arm. "Hey, I'm getting a glass of wine. Claudie, you want one?" Brynn knew better than to ask me. I hadn't touched a drop of anything since the night I got sick.

"No, thanks," Claudette answered. "Summer comes from a dirt-poor family, you know. Like, not having enough to eat poor, no shoes in the winter, no electricity, coal miner's daughter poor."

"How do you know?" Brynn asked.

"I met her sister once, when she first came here. I thought it was her mom. She's got like twelve brothers and sisters or something. It explains a lot, like why, when she goes home, there's no address to send her checks to. Just a P.O. box she has to drive to."

"Why wouldn't she give out her address?" I asked.

"Because where she lives it's so remote the mailman doesn't even go there."

"Oh."

"Well, there is some good news for you, Allee," Brynn said, giving me another punch.

"Ouch. What?"

"Less mess for you to clean up."

"Yeah," says Claudette. "And now you can sleep on the lower bu—"

She was about to say "bunk." But the word got stuck in her throat.

Because a trickle of blood was seeping out of Brynn's nose.

chapter ⑲

I talked to Brynn that day, like Momma wanted me to. Claudette did too. Brynn got really angry at first, called us names, flipped over the coffee table. Later, she agreed she needed to get her coke habit under control. She really seemed to turn over a new leaf too. I was starting to like her more. I thought she'd gone off the stuff. She probably did, for a while.

My modeling really took off in March. In this business, when things started happening, they happened fast. The national commercial for Taboo got me into the Screen Actors Guild and entitled me to residual checks. After I did Taboo, I got another national for Dentyne Ice gum and a regional for Florida Power & Light. In April, I flew to Costa Rica for a deodorant commercial and Mexico for a shampoo commercial, and had a few print jobs in between. The money was coming in.

By April, I was the "It" model in Miami for commercials this season, even though I'd come on the scene late. Casting directors called to request me, sometimes e-mailing agencies for an "Allee Rose" type. I could have left the apartment and gotten my own place if I'd wanted to. I was making more than Claudette or Brynn.

My passport was filling up with stamps, my chart was filling up with options, my agenda was filling up with voucher receipts and Polaroids from jobs. Still, I wasn't making the really big bucks the fashion types got from beauty campaigns, like cosmetics and fragrance. April the Great booked a perfume campaign for some insanely huge amount of money, like six figures, a real feat these days considering celebrities usually book a lot of that stuff. And I didn't get any magazine covers like Summer did.

Summer. Yech. I could barf just thinking about her.

Anyway, I was in this for the money, and I had a good, solid stream of payment coming in. The agency advanced some of it because it took print clients thirty to ninety days for clients to pay. If the Taboo and Dentyne Ice spots ran as much as the clients said they would, I would make great money.

Honestly, though, it wasn't about the money or Yale anymore. It wasn't even about trying to beat Brynn and Summer at their own game, even though that's exactly what I did. Brynn had tried to psych me out when I first got here, and then Summer tried to sabotage me when she realized I was her biggest competition. But it didn't work, either time. That victory wasn't what excited me, though.

What excited me was the job itself. I was really into it. I liked moving in front of the camera, feeling beautiful, seeing myself in pictures and on TV. And the competitive part of me lived for that *yessss-I-did-it* feeling of nailing a casting and then finding out I beat the other girls out and booked the job. I even liked the camaraderie I had with Brynn and Claudette and all the other models I was competing against. Back home, I'd been so wrapped up in my routine of intense studying, after-school activities, and working, I had never slowed down and just hung out with people. Now I did that all the time. I relaxed at the apartment talking to Claudette or Brynn, if she wasn't out with Luca, or I met Miguel at the News Cafe. At castings and even jobs, most of the time we models sat around waiting and talking, just chilling out.

I liked having friends.

And for all my feminism and academic achievement, I was a sucker for this business.

I felt like a star and I loved it.

We were in the conference room so we could watch my Taboo commercial. The advertising agency had e-mailed it to Finesse and Miguel was putting it up on the computer. Momma, Kate, Claudette, Brynn, and even Monique were all sitting around the table. Monique had just finished telling everyone about her Botox treatment this morning, which explained why she looked like a glazed robot. Oh, good, it was starting.

There I was, wandering in the jungle (Fairchild Tropical Gardens), wearing a two-piece outfit made of leaves (fabric with leaves glued on). The guy who got booked with me (Blake didn't get it) was behind me. Our footsteps crunched on the leaves and

205

branches. The sounds of rattlesnakes and jungle animals surrounded us. Then we saw cans of Taboo, growing out of a bush. Our faces were full of surprise and joy. He took one, drank with gusto while I watched, smiling. Then the techno blips and bleeps of dance music took over and the screen was filled with me doing a dance of happiness.

Or what was supposed to be a dance of happiness. Or what was supposed to be a dance. Or a sane movement by someone not demented.

Okay, I knew I might be bad, but this was . . . this was . . .

Oh, God.

Everyone was in hysterics. Claudette was bent in half. Miguel was choking on his Pepsi. Momma's jowls were quivering with laughter. Monique's face was statue-still. Or she could have been smiling. It was hard to tell.

The recorded voice-over was loud and clear: "In some cultures, girls are forbidden from dancing." Cut to a close-up of the guy's stunned face. Then there was a freeze-frame on me in a totally uncoordinated move with my butt going one way and the rest of me going the other way, my eyes rolling up into my head (how did that happen???), my mouth squinched up worse than when Abuela didn't have her teeth in.

Voice-over: "Maybe some girls *should* be forbidden from dancing."

OH. MY. GOD.

I AM SO EMBARRASSED.

I *knew* I'd sucked at the casting. I *knew* it. I knew it I knew it I knew it. But they booked me anyway.

Of course. Of course they did. Because they obviously wanted someone who really sucked! And I was perfect! Because I sucked! I blew! I couldn't dance. Not even a little bit. Not even remotely.

Now it was the house party scene and God help me, I was trying to drink Taboo and bust a move at the same time. While all the extras around me were busting a gut. I remembered now the director ordering them to "Laugh! Laugh!" But I just thought he meant laugh like have a good time laugh, like in those wine commercials where people were at a cocktail party chuckling and having fun. No, he meant laugh, specifically, at *me*.

Summer was right. There *were* all kinds of smart and all kinds of stupid. And I was some kind of stupid, all right. My cheeks must have been as red as my M•A•C Viva Glam lipstick.

The voice-over ended the commercial with: "Taboo. Not forbidden."

And it was over.

As was my commercial streak after this.

Because now I was finished. Finito. Done. Toast.

"Allee, you are so talented," Monique said.

WHAT DID SHE JUST SAY?

"So talented," she said again. "You're a natural comedienne. Imagine, I thought you had no personality when you first came here." She looked at Momma. "It's always the quiet ones."

"We have to get her reel together right away," Momma says.

"I think I wet myself," Kate sputtered, still laughing.

"Yeah," Brynn said. "Forget Yale. You should be on *Saturday Night Live*."

Miguel was wiping tears from his eyes. "*Qué cómica*, you are so funny. I didn't know you could do physical comedy. Why didn't you ever tell us?"

They thought I was acting. That I'd *tried* to suck. Because nobody could be that bad naturally. Except, of course, me.

I cleared my throat. "I didn't know I could either."

Claudette was the only one not saying anything. She just gave me a kitty-cat smile and winked. And after everyone was out of compliments and we were filing out of the conference room, Claudette whispered in my ear, "Babygirl, you are a rhythmless nation. But don't worry, your secret is safe with me."

I got recognized all the time. People stopped me in the street and asked me to do the dance. I didn't, though. I'd never dance in public again. Unless, of course, they made another spot using me, and it was looking like they might because this commercial was a huge hit, the kind that everyone talked about. *Deco Drive*, Miami's local gossip show, featured me in an interview. Momma wanted to put the TV interview on my reel, along with my commercials. Dad called and said someone he worked with asked if the funny Taboo girl was his daughter. Imagine me, having a rep as a funny girl! Me, of the former Queen Serious, Wednesday Addams rep.

It took me a while to realize I was funny. I mean, I knew everyone else thought I was funny, but I was secretly super-duper embarrassed. After all, I was the butt of a joke. Miguel noticed I wasn't laughing one night while he was over watching a "Which one is the guy?" drag queen modeling contest on *The Tyra Banks Show* with me. It was a commercial break, and then there I was, dancing in the jungle, freeze-framed in all my royal spazziness. So I confessed that I didn't think it was funny, that I wasn't acting, and that I really dance like that when no one's around. I had to give him props because he didn't ask to watch me dance. He just stared at me for a few seconds, shrugged one shoulder, and said, "*No importa*. If you can't laugh at yourself, laugh at other people," and we went back to making fun of the tacky drag queens.

I was starting to laugh at myself now, though. There was no doubt about it, I did look hilarious. I *had* to laugh at myself. Not for being a rhythmless nation, which, it was painfully obvious to me now, I totally was, but for being so clueless, for not realizing why they'd booked me. How could I have been so stupid, not to see where they were going with me? Obviously, I was not the Jane Brain I thought I was.

But you know what? It was okay. Because, apparently, I had other good qualities. I was a pretty good commercial model. And a pretty good print model. And a pretty good friend.

From now on, I was going to try not to take myself, and everything, so seriously. Of course, it was easy for me to say that since I wasn't in school, worrying about test scores and papers I had to write. But I did take the WHAT WOULD WEDNESDAY ADDAMS DO? bumper sticker off my car. The Taboo commercial and everybody's reaction to it had me thinking that there was something to be said for lightening up.

"You better stay away from him, or you're going in," I said angrily with my hands on my hips.

"Go ahead," Brynn shot back, stepping closer to me in her metallic bikini. "I've got my Seagull on." We locked eyes and got closer, almost nose to nose. But as hard as we tried to concentrate and keep a straight face, we just couldn't. It was too funny. We lost it. The director was not amused. We had to rehearse it again.

This was the first time Brynn and I had worked together. It was a commercial for Seagull waterproof suntan lotion. We'd just finished the first scene where the extras were dancing and we were all pretending to have a great time at this poolside barbecue. The director was playing Black Eyed Peas to get us wilding out. I was in a red-and-white-checkered half shirt with denim shorts. The only drama so far was that the director had screamed at the stylist because my shirt matched the tablecloths and they weren't supposed to, so they removed the tablecloths.

"Just don't push me too hard," Brynn warned me. "These bottoms are loose and they'll fall right off."

"Good," I said. "You'll get a higher rate for nudity." Her bottoms looked like they might fall off anyway, she'd gotten so thin. She was starting to get that heroin chic look that was so in style in the nineties.

"Not a bad idea. Hey, I'm taking a ciggie break with the crew. Be right back." She got a light from a gaffer, and I was amazed at how friendly she was with the crew. None of the other talent talked to the crew. I was scared of them. Some of the electrical technicians looked like they'd done hard time in prison, and the others bore a resemblance to Comic Book Guy from *The Simpsons*.

They turned the music off when they were ready to shoot the next scene. "Action!" That was my cue to walk alongside the pool holding hands with this hot guy who had great cheekbones (think younger David Beckham). He and I were acting all goony-eyed with each other until Brynn came into the scene, strutting by with a hot dog in her hand. Young David, distracted by Brynn, lifted his eyes off me to check her out. Brynn gave him a sizzling look as she bit into her hot dog. I then stepped in front of him and made my expression go from goody-goody girlfriend to royally possessive girlfriend.

"Cut!" Time to do it again. Brynn took this opportunity to spit out her hot dog. We did a few more takes, and every time, she spit it out into a napkin, refusing to swallow even one bite. A bottle of Crystal Light was all she'd had today. I honestly didn't know how she stayed alive.

Next came the fun part, where I had to say to Brynn, "You better back off, or you're going in."

"Go ahead. I've got my Seagull on." I looked at her forehead, not her eyes, or we'd lose it again. Concentrate, we were rolling . . . no laughing . . . count 1 . . . 2 . . . and push! She fell back with a cute splash.

"Cut!" Everyone clapped. The director, the crew, the extras, everybody. Poor Brynn. She had to go back to hair and makeup now so we could do it all over again.

"Oh, man, it's gonna take forever till the next take," said one of the extras.

"Nice. Now we'll get overtime," another one answered.

I reached down to help her out, but the stylist yelled at me, worried I'd get my clothes wet. Who cared? The hair and makeup guy could just blow-dry it out. Honestly, everyone thought models and actors were so difficult, but the truth was that we had the least issues compared to everybody else in the business.

We did it a few more times and Brynn and I didn't crack up once, proving we were pros. She and I high-fived each other when it was all done. Things had changed a lot between us, probably starting with the day I caught her crying. And she was in a good mood most of the time. She seemed pretty clean these days.

Hopefully, we'd work together again before I had to go back home in a few weeks. The end of season was near, and everybody would be going off somewhere. The difference was that they were all going to exciting places like Paris and Milan to do the fall/winter shows, while I was going to Cape Vomit for summer school. It would be weird leaving all this. At least I'd be at Yale in a few months. It all seemed a million years away, when really, it was around the corner.

I waited in my car for Brynn while she was in the bathroom. This commercial was just a limited-run regional, so it wouldn't be that much money, but it would look good for my reel. It showed I could handle dialogue and a principal part.

Where was Brynn? She'd been gone a long time. She'd said she just had to pee. I'd better see if she was okay.

The crew was still disassembling equipment and packing up. I found the door to the cabana bathroom and knocked. "Just a sec." It was Brynn. She came out, sniffing, moving her nose around. One of the crew guys came out behind her.

They'd been snorting coke.

The guy walked away, and Brynn and I had a stare-off. I won. She looked away first, then started walking toward the car. "So, you wanna hit Glitter tonight with me and Luca? They're having free Roberto Cavalli cocktails. Oh, yeah, that's right, you don't drink. Anyway, I got passes. And I'll let you borrow my Dolce & Gabbana jeans, the ones you like, the white ones with the gold letters."

"No, thanks. I'll pass."

I loved Ocean Drive first thing in the morning, when it was getting ready for the day. Chairs and tables were being set up at outdoor cafés, striped awnings were being rolled out, sidewalks hosed down. Halter-top-wearing hostesses were taking their posts with clipboards in hand, and soft classical music was playing on one block, then drowned out by salsa music on another.

The agency was still eight blocks away, but I had to stop first at the Marlin hotel to get Brynn. We both had to meet with our bookers and we wanted to go in together. She'd just called to say they were about to wrap her commercial. I was glad she'd made it to her booking. She had never come home from Glitter last night.

I bladed to the Marlin without falling. It was a cool, retro deco hotel with a rock 'n' roll atmosphere. The crew was outside on the front terrace. It was an exterior scene, so I could watch from across the street. I sat on a bench next to an old lady with peach-colored helmet hair. There was a sliver of space in between the equipment and the crew where I could see everything. Brynn was coming down the top steps in a sequined mini and tube top, hanging on the arm of some guy in tight jeans. She lost her balance and he pulled her back up. The director said, "Cut." She crumpled down on the steps and rested her head in her hands.

I heard Luca's motorcycle before I saw it. He pulled up to the curb in front of my bench, his bike chugging and jumping. I swear that thing was a live animal. The lady next to me clutched her purse with both hands. I didn't blame her. He looked scuzzier than Ewan McGregor did in that movie *Trainspotting* right after he crawled out of the toilet. "She come home last night?" he asked. We were both looking at Brynn, crumpled on the steps.

"No. I thought she was with you."

His lizard face looked worried. Brynn did the scene a couple of times, finally got it right, then collapsed on the steps again. I heard the director call, "We're wrapped," and I Rollerbladed over there. Luca followed on his bike.

Brynn fell on me. "Well, that wuzzaz fun as a sandpaper enema," she slurred into my shoulder. She smelled like smoke and alcohol.

"Hey, biatch, where ya been?" Luca called from his bike. "Lemme take you back to my place."

Her bloodshot eyes went all soft at the sight of him, proving that love is blind. She blew him a wobbly kiss. "Wait here. I'll get my bag."

"She's got a meeting at the agency," I told him while she was inside.

"Tell 'em she's sick. She's gotta sleep it off." I hesitated. "Go on. I'll take care of her."

And then it hit me. I'd told Momma and Kate that Brynn wouldn't listen to anybody, but that wasn't true. There was one person she listened to, one person who cared about her more than anyone.

And it wasn't Luca.

Someone had to call Brynn's mother soon, before it was too late.

It's no use going back to yesterday,
because I was a different person then.

chapter (20)

My parents finally got me to go home for a weekend. Cape Comet had a smell. Not a bad one, really. It was like salt, rust, and wood all rolled into one. I had the window open so I was getting a really good whiff of it, driving into town. A pickup truck full of fishing gear was passing me. So were cars with Kennedy Space Center license plates. I turned onto our street just as an Air Force plane flew above me with a loud roar.

I was home.

Mom, Dad, Abuela, and Robby rushed out of the house when I got out of the car. Mom hugged me and put her hands on my cheeks. "Omigod, Allee, look at your hair, your makeup! Are you wearing heels? You are! I can't get over it," and on and on. Then

Dad hugged me. "There she is, the TV star," he said all proudly. Abuela was next. She had three words for me. "You're too thin." Robby just wrapped himself around my leg. He'd gotten so big!

Where was Sabrina? I was hoping she'd be the first to welcome me back, not the last. It was her I'd been thinking of the whole drive here. I was wearing the dress she'd made. I picked up Robby and carried him into the house.

And there she was. Standing in the family room, waiting for me. Wearing the necklace I'd sent her. Her hand flew up to her throat, adjusting it. It matched her eyes, just like I knew it would. Except her eyes were looking a little more red than violet right now.

I knew how she felt; my eyes were tearing up too.

"Look, Sabrina," Robby said. "It's Allee." I put him down and did a little twirl. She didn't say anything.

"So?" I asked.

She wiped her eyes and said, "It's a little dressy for daytime, don't you think?"

And then we hugged. Hard.

My room looked different now. Sabrina's sewing stuff was everywhere. My bed was covered with fabric and hand-drawn patterns, and the desk was a mess of scissors, spools of thread, pattern books, buttons, pins, and zippers. How could she afford all this? And how did she find anything in this sty? It was worse than our apartment in Miami Beach. I'd have to clean some of this up later.

She was on her bed, flipping through my portfolio. I was changing into jeans and a halter top. "Hard to believe you were ever fashionably challenged," she murmured, turning a page.

216

"Why'd they put you in a beret and cowboy boots? You never mix western with French."

"Good to know. What'd you think of my Taboo commercial?"

"Allee, I told you you couldn't dance. What were you thinking?"

"I always thought you were teasing."

"People at school do their own version of it, like, imitating you. They're always asking me if I knew you were so funny. You know, because you were such an egghead in school and all."

"Take a look in the back." She did, and pulled out the issue of *Dietra* magazine that I was in. "The client sent some copies to the agency this week. Take a look."

She flipped a few pages and then her eyebrows shot up. I knew which picture she was looking at. "Omigod, Allee, look at you." She wasn't smiling.

"You don't like it?" I asked, stunned.

She looked up at me. "I love it."

I breathed a sigh of relief. Her opinion was important to me. "Keep it if you want. I've got another copy."

"Your body looks hot. Wow, if you look close, you can see your—"

"I know, I know, don't remind me. And hide it before Dad sees it and has a heart attack," I said, lacing up my wedge espadrilles. "So what else is going on around here?"

"Nothing, as usual. They opened up a Piggly Wiggly next to the coin laundry. Oh, and guess what? Some kids have actually, like, bought the clothes I made. Hillary paid forty bucks for one just like the one I sent you, but in red. I'm, like, taking orders."

"Sabrina, that's so awesome," I said, brushing my hair. "You know, you could charge two hundred for that dress."

"In Cape Comet? Keep dreaming. But maybe someday."

"What's someday? You want to open a store? I thought you wanted to be a model."

She chewed her lip, hesitating. "I never wanted to be a model." I stopped brushing. Was she joking? "I *thought* I wanted to be a model, but now I realize I didn't."

"Then what the hell were you not speaking to me for?" I yelled. I held up my brush, poised to throw it at her.

"It was always the clothes I was into. Designing and making clothes made me see that. I want to be a designer. It's, like, my passion."

I tossed the brush on her bed and sat next to her. "I think that's great, Sabrina. Really."

"Do you think I'm good enough? As a designer, I mean?"

I glanced around at all her sewing stuff on my bed. "You're more than good. Everybody always asks me about that blue dress, and you should see their faces when I tell them my sister designed it."

Her eyes got all misty again. "Really?"

I looked away. This wasn't easy to say. "I owe you an apology."

"What for?"

"I used to think that because you were so into fashion that, well . . ." I knocked on my head. "I sorta thought you didn't have much going on upstairs. I even called you The Fluff. Secretly. To myself."

"Pretty and stupid." She raised her eyebrows. "Right?"

I nodded. I guess I had stereotyped her. "Pretty and smart. I was wrong. And I'm sorry."

"You do that to a lot of people, you know."

"What?"

"Put them in, like, a category. The Fluff. Hillary High Beams. What do you call my friends? Trendy Wendies? You don't even know them. You even put yourself in a category. You're"—she made quote marks with her fingers—"the smart one."

I thought about that.

The Fluff . . . Hillary High Beams . . .

Maybe it was true.

Okay, it was. I did do that to people. Especially Sabrina. And I'd always purposely avoided fashion and beauty because I wanted to make sure people knew I was smart. Like if I was too girly I wouldn't be taken seriously or something. As if beauty and intelligence were mutually exclusive. How stupid was that? And the worst part was, I knew I would have enjoyed hanging out with Mom and Sabrina more, going clothes shopping or watching a show about beauty secrets or whatever. Instead, I was too busy trying to make a point. A point that was wrong. Way wrong.

It sucked to admit crappy stuff about yourself.

Sabrina closed my portfolio. "And calling her Hillary High Beams? That sounds like something a pig like Jake or Scott would call her, not someone who says she's, like, a feminist or whatever."

I thought about that one too.

Maybe I'd take a women's studies course at Yale.

chapter ㉑

Since season was winding down, the agency had time for open calls. There was an army of overlipsticked wannabe models in the lobby. I held the door open for two girls walking in. "If they don't want me," one of them said, "then frankly, I question their taste."

Bonnie, the high-security receptionist who'd crushed my confidence the first time I came here, buzzed me in now without a word. I clicked past the wannabes in my Bottega Veneta pumps and Elie Tahari blouse, and I could feel them sizing me up. Some recognized me from my Taboo spot, and probably from Dentyne Ice too. I could tell by the whispers. I held my head up high, smiled graciously. It was a long way from Cape Comet, and I wasn't beige anymore.

I sat next to Momma, Kate, and Dimitri in front of Monique's desk. Monique was eating a bagel with plenty of cream cheese. It was nice to know her facial muscles were back in working order. "Allee, I'm going to cut right to the chase," she said with her mouth full. Agents didn't waste time with small talk. They always got right to the big talk. "There's an agency in Japan that's very interested in you. We want you to consider going for the summer season there."

"Excuse me?" I could never understand anyone when their mouth was full.

She swallowed and said, "Agence, an agency in Tokyo, wants to us to place you with them for the summer."

"Tokyo, Japan?"

"Ye-e-es. Tokyo, Japan."

"It would mean a lot of money for you, sweetie," said Momma. "There's a lot of TV work there. Agence saw your reel and fell in love with you. And it would be the experience of a lifetime."

"You would do very well in the Japanese market," said Dimitri. "They don't like them too tall."

"Oh," said Monique, jumping a little in her seat as if she'd just thought of something. "We have to put five eight on your card, not five nine. In Japan, you want to go more petite."

"I can't go to Japan," I told them. "I have to finish high school this summer."

"You could go right after that or get a GED," said Dimitri. Me? Get a GED? I almost laughed in his face.

"But I'm going to Yale in the fall. That's why I started modeling, for the extra money I needed to pay for it."

"Yale will always be there, sweetie," said Momma. "Tokyo is a now-or-never deal, and you can bet your ass it's the experience of a lifetime."

"But I was planning on going to college."

Monique chomped on her bagel, looked at Dimitri and Momma. "Look, we can't stop her from going to college, especially Yale." Monique swallowed, looked back at me, wiping her hands on a napkin. "Listen, there are girls desperate to go to Japan. Do whatever you want, Allee."

"Just think about it," Kate said.

There was nothing to think about. They were all waiting for some kind of response from me. I was curious about one thing. "How can I work for another agency? I thought I was exclusive with Finesse."

"We're your mother agency," said Momma. "When our season is over, we place you with another agency in a different market, then you come back to us in the fall."

"Oh. Well, I don't think I can do it. Especially in Japan. Aren't they a really sexist society? I'm sort of a feminist. I don't think I could live there."

That got a flat-out laugh from Kate. "What kind of flipping feminist are you? Aren't you forgetting you posed showing some of your naughty bits in tiny knickers and a weensie bra?"

"I didn't show any naughty bits!" I sort of shouted.

"Almost. Look at the picture. It's a matter of centimeters, love. Centimeters."

I was trembling like a Chihuahua. I'd never really yelled at an adult like that before. Man, this assertiveness thing could get out of control if you weren't careful. But Kate was pissing me off. It wasn't as if I'd posed for *Playboy*. It wasn't as if I'd stopped having feminist values. I'd just posed scantily clad *in spite of* my values.

Or something.

Monique clasped her hands on her desk, leaned toward me. "Allee, do you realize you're in the one business dominated by *women*, controlled by *women*, where *women* categorically make more money than men?"

"Yeah." I glanced at Kate and had to admit, "By exploiting their bodies, I guess."

Monique leaned forward even more, one eye glinting at me. "Celebrating their bodies, not exploiting. You say you're sort of a feminist. Isn't a big part of feminism supposed to be about taking ownership of your body, feeling good about it and saying *vagina* over and over and all of that?" Nobody moved. I couldn't believe she'd just said *vagina*. "What's the difference between that and celebrating your body in a picture, an artfully done photograph?"

Um. I honestly didn't know. I'd never thought about it like that.

Monique threw her hands up. "If that's not feminism, then I don't know what is."

I didn't know either anymore. I was very confused.

Monique sighed and her lips went tight, a feat I didn't think possible. "Just think about Japan," she said.

"Okay." As I opened the door to leave, I looked back at them and said, "Thank you for the opportunity." I had learned some things from Summer. And the truth was, it *was* an incredible opportunity. For someone else.

Just not me. Because I had other goals, and I'd never wanted to be a model in the first place. Even though the idea of modeling in an exciting foreign country, making tons of money, having great adventures and experiences was like winning the lottery for some people, it wasn't for me. Because I was headed for an Ivy League future.

Period.

Miguel was at his desk. It had slowed down a lot in the booking room. Just two weeks ago this room had a tense atmosphere, with the bookers glued to their interconnected desks, talking into headsets, and staring at their screens with such concentration I wondered if somehow they were stopping a nuclear reactor from detonating instead of booking pretty girls and pretty boys in pretty pictures.

But right now it was very relaxed. One of the bookers was cutting old composite cards and making finger puppets. The bookers were having a bash-and-trash session. They must have forgotten I was in the room, listening.

"You could land a plane on that forehead."

"That's not a forehead, that's a fivehead."

"Check the new girl, Maria K. She's got that it's going to be very expensive to hook up with me look."

"Yeah, you'd never know that in Nicaragua she was sorting coffee beans for pennies a day, wearing one of those sad little kerchiefs on her head."

I whispered to Miguel, "What do they say when I'm not around?"

"I can't tell you because that would be unprofessional. But walk on my back and I just might. Oh, by the way, I think I've found your ticket."

"You found my ticket and you didn't tell me?"

"I have to show you, not tell you. Let's pull up your e-book." He clicked the Lifestyle icon on his computer and all the models on Finesse's commercial board appeared, including me. He clicked on my image and photos from my portfolio appeared. The lingerie shot for *Dietra* was the first one. "Here we go." He snapped his fingers, swayed in his seat. "She's a sexy supah stah, yeah . . ."

"Stop," I said. All of Uta Scholes's pictures popped with feeling and surreal visuals. Miguel clicked on the shot of me lying across the blanket in the Gaultier tutu, with the boy and the bunnies. It looked like a painting. So much had gone into this photo, so many talents. All of us—me, the boy, the crew—made that image together. We all had a part in bringing the vision to life, like the cast of a play, almost. I was totally wrong about fashion photography not being art. It was, sometimes. I was even starting to see some of the clothing as art. What was the difference if you hung it on a person or a wall? A creation was a creation.

"I love, love, love this shot," said Miguel, pointing to my lingerie shot. "It's *perfecto dilecto*. The sunset, your skin, your shape."

"I still don't know how I booked that."

"I don't know either," said Dimitri.

Miguel slapped his hand on his desk and shouted at Dimitri, "That is so mean!" He turned to me. "She's so bitchy today, she's driving me up the wall." It took me a sec to realize the "she" he was referring to was Dimitri.

And Dimitri didn't like it. "I am not being bitchy today, but if I am, it's because you took my last farking pencil, you little thief. I said I don't know how she booked that because she's not edgy enough."

The bookers all weighed in on this topic. "That's why they booked her, because the very idea of edgy is doing the unexpected."

"And what could be more unexpected than taking a commercial girl, edging her up, and putting her in a fashion editorial?"

"You're right, that *is* edgy."

"The essence of edgy."

I didn't want Miguel to lose his focus on me. "Excuse me, but could we get back to my ticket?"

Miguel turned back to the computer and clicked on another of my pictures. It was an ad for Viva deodorant, a still taken from the commercial I'd done in Costa Rica. It was an *hommage* to Amelia Earhart. I was standing next to an antique propeller plane with an old-fashioned flight helmet on, leather jacket, and slouchy pants. Next was a test shot of me gazing out from a rooftop and another where I was driving a speedboat with some guys in the backseat.

"Were you really driving that?" Miguel asked.

"No, it wasn't even moving." There was a catalog tear sheet from an athletic-wear catalog where I was running away from the camera and looking back with a playful smile, my hair flying out wildly in the wind as I was being chased by a guy. I really liked the Latina Allee pictures from my first test shoot. I was sitting outside, sipping Cuban café out of a little cup, touching the flowers in my hair. I remembered trying to take them out because there were bugs biting my scalp. The last picture was at the beach, and I was screaming "Whee!" in a bathing suit. It was at an angle, and my rear end was jutting out, high and round.

Miguel was watching me, not the screen. "Do you see your ticket?"

226

It might have been my legs or hair, but models with great hair and legs were a dime a dozen, so that couldn't be it. I really hoped it wasn't . . . "My butt?"

"No." He laughed.

"My hair?"

"No. Your ticket isn't physical."

"What? How could it not be physical?"

"It's what shows up in the pictures, *niña,* and what shows up in the pictures is your attitude."

"I have an attitude?"

"You do, a good one. *Mira,* look at this." He clicked onto an extreme close-up of my face, known as a beauty shot. There was a burning look in my eyes. "See? A client looks at that and goes, 'There's a lot going on in that pretty head.'"

"I don't see it. What are you saying? My ticket is my intelligence?"

"Well, I don't know how intelligent you are if you can't see your ticket."

"Miguel, just say what it is already."

He inhaled, exhaled, smoothed back his hair. "You're versatile and you have a range of looks, like a model should, but you're bringing more than just personality to the table. In every picture, you're a strong girl, someone smart, in charge of herself. There isn't one shot where a guy is dominating you or where you're just standing there, even when the client has another guy in the shot."

"But I did do a couple of jobs with guys where it looks like that."

"We didn't put them in your book. Those aren't your strongest shots, probably because you're not comfortable with the pretty plaything role. Your ticket, *mi amor*, is your approach that girls—*perdón*—women aren't just objects of beauty."

"So my ticket is my point of view?"

"*Sí*. It's unique, especially around here. It's what makes you you, and it shows in your pictures. I don't know how, but it's there."

That was extremely cool. In fact, that was the best ticket I could have hoped for, and by far, a better ticket than anyone else had. I smiled at Miguel, and it wasn't my casting smile, it was a real one. "Thank you. I wouldn't have figured that out on my own."

"I know. You can't even figure out how to coordinate. Look at your shoes and purse. But if you want to thank me, I'll let you walk on my back."

"Bravo, Allee," Dimitri said, patting me on the head like a dog. Excuse me, had he heard anything Miguel had just said? "And bravo, Miguel. You explain it so good. This is why you work for me. Not like those two, who don't work for anybody." I followed his gaze toward the glass wall that looked out into the lobby. Irina and Vlada were going into Monique's office. They were wearing waitress uniforms.

"They're working at some new restaurant that's opening on Washington tonight," Miguel said. "They said they'd come by and drop off party passes. They must be getting paid under the table."

"At least they'll be getting paid somewhere," said Dimitri.

I couldn't get over how exquisite they were, like two mythological goddesses, even in those waitress uniforms. "Why didn't they ever get booked?" I wondered out loud.

"Their pictures had no feeling," said Dimitri. "No nothing. Cold. In photos, they had no life."

228

Miguel nodded. "No ticket."

It was nice to know *I* had one.

"You should go to Japan," Sabrina said after I'd told her about the Japan offer.

"You think so?"

"Totally. Fashion is so wild over there."

I sighed. "I wish I could go."

"Are you impaired? Why can't you? I would die to go to Japan."

"They said the money is really good too."

"Then why wouldn't you go?"

"Because my goal was always Yale, not Tokyo. Besides, it's too crazy. And what about finishing summer school? Hello, graduating."

"So take your courses online from Tokyo. If you could do it from Miami, you could do it from Tokyo."

That was true. I hadn't thought about that.

"Change your goal," Sabrina said. "Go to Yale later."

I was at Intermix, trying on an Ella Moss wrap dress. I'd add it to the rest of what I was buying—Gucci sunglasses, a Red Carter bikini with an art deco architecture pattern on it, and a Chloé T-shirt for Sabrina. I only had another two weeks here, so I was getting in as much glam and fashion splurging as I could.

It was all expensive, and I knew every penny I made should go toward college, but this would be my big clothing splurge before summer school. Besides, those residual checks were coming in. Plus I figured this was also my reward for standing under hot lights for two hours this morning. It was an indoor shoot for a South American jeans company's online look book, and even though the rate was low, the client had given me three pairs of jeans to take home.

South Beach was starting to feel empty, quieter than usual. It would be time for me to go soon. I should be excited to finish summer school and go to Yale already.

So why wasn't I excited? I'd learn from the best of the best, be at the center of academic life, get to hang out with other kids who liked to study and read like me, maybe meet some hot, brilliant guy who'd sweep me off my feet. I'd fit in there, way better than I'd ever fit in here or in Comet. But then images jumped into my mind, of me walking through crowded Tokyo streets, of modeling in a Japanese runway show, of learning the language, traveling, maybe hanging out with Gwen Stefani and her Japanese girl posse. That whole Japan offer was really toying with my imagination.

But, of course, I couldn't take it. I'd always been Yale bound. I had to stick to the plan, not get sidetracked. Which was why I had to mail Yale my letter accepting their offer already. I had been waiting until I was sure I'd have the money, and I did now.

So what was I waiting for? This was what I'd always wanted.

"Hey, aren't you the girl from the Taboo commercial, the one who dances so funny?" It was the salesgirl.

"Yes." I smiled.

"Oh, you are so hilarious. I didn't recognize you at first. Do you want me to ring that stuff up for you?"

"No," I said. "I want to stay awhile. I'm not quite finished . . . shopping."

• • •

It was Thursday night and Dimitri's facial stubble and tousled hair were looking ferociously hot this evening. I was sitting with him and Miguel at Nobu, at a tiny square table in the bar area. We were waiting for Claudette so we could get a big table in the dining room. Brynn was supposed to show up too, but I wasn't counting on it.

This restaurant was the most on-the-scene restaurant on the scene. It was in the Shore Club, and there was no sign that said Nobu anywhere, not in the hotel, not on the garden terrace, not even on the door to the restaurant. You were supposed to just know where it was, like an only those in the know can know kind of thing. It was dark with tons of candles, and it was model central. Everyone was striking poses, hair-tossing and eye-flirting. Miguel not only knew who half the room was, he could dish about them.

"Okay, time for dis and tell. That's Paula, thinks she's a model and she so isn't, *puro* deadweight, but her boyfriend is John Singer, you know, the photographer? So the agency signed her to get John's business. And that's Julie Marshand. 'Member her, Dimitri? We used to rep her for lifestyle. She was a high-class escort back in the day, before she married the real estate king Chaim Ludevitch. *Ay Dios*, Paula's coming over, don't look."

Paula came over and Dimitri did his whole kissing-on-both-cheeks bit. And then I glanced down and screeched to a halt, almost dropping my Coke. *Dimitri's hand was clasped firmly in Miguel's.* How long had this been going on? I thought they were strictly a working duo.

In the middle of fumbling with his chopsticks and sushi, Miguel noticed I'd noticed. "Allee, will you keep it on the down low? It just started, and we're trying to keep it private."

"Sure, but . . ."

"What?"

"He drives you up the wall. You said so yourself."

"Oh, that." He waved his free hand. "He does, but that's just his office personality, when he's stressed. He's different when we're alone."

"Should you be dating your boss? All the magazines say you shouldn't."

"Which is why you have to shut up about it." I mimed locking up my lips and throwing away the key. "Look, he needs me and . . . I think I love him. I just realized it. Sometimes a person is right in front of you and you don't really see them, you know?"

"I know. My sister's been right in front of me my whole life, but I never really saw her for who she is until I left home. It took being away from her for me to understand her." I sipped my Coke, thinking about the parade of mistaken identities that had marched through my life since January. I'd thought Summer was genuine and sweet when she was dangerously toxic. Brynn had some problems, but she wasn't mean or out for my blood, like I first thought. She was just brutally honest and thought life should be a party. And what about Claudette? I wrote her off as a primo weirdo when I met her. Her train was a little off the tracks, it was true, but she was one of the warmest, most intelligent, open-minded people I'd ever met. I'd been wrong about a lot of people who'd been right in front of me. "Does Dimitri love you?"

He nodded and actually looked embarrassed. I bet if it wasn't so dark in here, I'd see him blushing. Paula left, and Dimitri turned to Miguel with this look of pure adoration. They were in their own world until Miguel screamed, "Omigod, is that Ricky Martin?!" It was, and after a while, we saw Pamela Anderson and after that, Mickey Rourke. "Look at Pam. She gives white trash a bad name, but you know what? I still love her. Poor Mickey, though. He looks like a science project. His face is more quilted than a Chanel bag. And what is that, is he carrying a dog? Ooh, do you see who I see? That's . . . oh, wait . . . no, that's Summer."

"Where?" Dimitri and I asked.

"Over there." She was with midlife crisis man, shaking hands with a group of people, looking every inch a movie star. The group left the bar, and she went with them into the dining room. "See the fat guy with the beard she just said hello to?"

"Yeah." He looked like a demented mountain man, the kind who kidnapped female joggers and took them for brides.

"He's a movie producer. Like, a really big deal in Australia. They were interviewing him on *Deco Drive* last night. He's here for some film festival."

Whatever. Good for Summer. I'd be traveling on a different path soon anyway, far away from this one. This had all turned out to be a learning experience, and Summer was part of it.

chapter 22

Miguel came over. He threw the covers off me. All I had on was my A WOMAN NEEDS A MAN LIKE A FISH NEEDS A BICYCLE T-shirt and underwear. I'd been in bed all day, tired out from a three-day job in Nassau. My flight had come in at two in the morning. It was probably my last job this season, a nonunion educational film. The pay was crap, but I got to swim with dolphins *and* stay at an amazing resort. I loved it, but after three days smiling underwater, I was exhausted. I pulled the covers back over me so Miguel would take the hint.

He didn't. "I know you're awake, Allee cat. Come on, you're missing the art deco festival."

"Miguel, I love you, but go away."

"No. You've been here all day, and I don't know how to tell you this, *niña*, but you need to take a shower. Badly." He opened the blinds, sat on my bed, and took out a Styrofoam box with Cuban pastries, *pastelitos de guayaba*.

"Mmmm, those smell good," I said, opening my eyes.

"*Coño*, Allee, when was the last time you brushed your teeth?"

I pulled the covers over my mouth. "Yesterday."

"Well, it's time for some Scope." He poured *café cubano* from a big Styrofoam cup into a tiny cup and handed it to me, then picked up my copy of *Pride and Prejudice* from the floor and dropped it on my bed. "I can't believe you read that for fun. You're not gonna have time to read in Japan, you know. You'll be too busy."

"Miguel, I am not going to Japan." He kept pushing me to go.

"Why not? If I was you I wouldn't even bother with Cape Caca for summer school. I'd get a GED and be on the next plane to Tokyo."

"People like me don't get GEDs. I've dedicated the last four years to school and my grades."

"Correction. Three and a half years. The last few months you've dedicated yourself to being a model."

"I got into Yale. I'm not giving that up. My modeling days are gonna be over soon."

"You don't mean that."

"Yeah, I do. I have to go to college."

"You don't *have* to do anything."

I sighed. He didn't get it. "Japan is not in the Allee plan, okay? It's, like, out of the question not to go to Yale. I would totally be letting my parents down if I blew off an Ivy League education to go to the other side of the world and model." I snorted. "You don't *not* go to Yale if you get in. Nobody does that."

"Are you nobody? Hmmph. My mistake. I always thought you were somebody." He tapped my head with my book. "Somebody who needs to learn that there's a lot of freedom in not caring what other people think."

"It's not that simple, Miguel. I wish it was, but it's not."

"It is simple. It sounds like you're just going to Yale to please your parents. Where's that mind of your own you're so proud of?"

"Please my parents? Believe me, they would rather I take a full scholarship to a school right here in Florida and stay close to home. They'd deny it, but I know it's true. Yale was always my idea."

"Oh, yeah? Then why haven't you sent Yale your letter saying you're going?"

Damn. I forgot he knew about that. I sipped my coffee and pretended to be watching the palm trees out the window. I didn't know why I still hadn't sent in my acceptance. I didn't have a good answer for Miguel, so I just shrugged and said, "Haven't gotten around to it, that's all."

"*Mentirosa!* Liar. Deep deep down, you don't want to go anymore. Japan is calling your name. Come on, you know you're thinking about it."

"I haven't *seriously* been thinking about it." Did fantasizing count as thinking about it?

He smoothed out my comforter. "You know, when I left home, I said good riddance, *no joda*, never looked back. It's time to show your new self to the world, try new experiences."

"I showed myself to the world. Didn't you see my lingerie edi-torial?" I said with a mouth full of *pastelito*.

"I'm serious," Miguel said. "College isn't going anywhere, *niña*. You can always get your degree. But in a couple of years, you'll be too old to go to Japan and make a ton, and I do mean a ton. You'll regret it if you don't go. Truth. Tokyo is a golden op-portunity."

"For other models."

"For anybody. And you'll look fantabulous in a kimono. Ex-cept why do geishas wear socks with those wooden sandals? I don't get it."

He had me smiling.

And wondering. Could I really just give up my Yale plan and go to Japan?

What if I did?

What if I were to, maybe not give up Yale, but postpone it. I could still go to Yale someday. Just not now. I could always reapply or get a deferral or something.

Couldn't I?

It just seemed like such a crazy thing to do.

But coming here seemed crazy at first too, didn't it?

"This is Yale you're talking about, Allee. Yale. You crazy, talking about running off to Japan?"

I totally didn't expect this reaction from Claudette, Miss Live Life and Be Free. We were sitting in the sand, watching the sun go down on the beach.

"I'm not saying I won't go," I told her. "I'm just saying I might not go *now*. I could put Yale on hold for a year."

"On hold. I was gonna put college on hold, model for a while, travel some, and then go back to school. But it didn't work out that way, now, did it?"

"So why don't you go back now?"

She smiled at me the way I smiled at Robby when he asked me something that was hard to explain. "What, and join a sorority? Live in a dorm, write papers? Not for me. I'm a gypsy. But you, you're different. You should go to college. Take it from me, Allee, one year turns into two years and then three and then you never go back." She put her hand on my shoulder and looked at me eye to eye. "Don't make the biggest mistake of your life. Go to Yale."

Go to Yale. Don't pass go, don't stop to collect two hundred dollars, just go straight to Yale. Play it safe.

But what if I didn't play it so safe? Would I end up like Claudette in a few years, living in a model apartment and still making the casting rounds? I mean, I could say that that wouldn't happen to me, that I'd only take a year off and I'd force myself to go back to school.

But what if that didn't happen?

What if I reached a point where I was beyond living in a dorm and going to class? Maybe you just can't get off the modeling road once you're on it for a while. Maybe if I went on traveling and modeling more and more, it would be too hard to walk away from the glamour, the good money, the excitement, the travel, the freedom.

It was hard to walk away from all that now.

Sabrina was on the phone. "Mom and Dad found the *Dietra* magazine."

"Sabrina! I told you to hide it."

"I did, but then I forgot where I hid it. Mom found it."

"Great, thanks a lot. What did she say?"

"Um, she's right here, bye."

"No, wait, I don't want to talk to—"

"That's some outfit you have on, Allee." Mom sounded mad, like the way she used to get on me if I was reading at the dinner table. "What will people think when they see this? Aren't you embarrassed?"

"No."

"Well, you should be. I'm embarrassed."

"Who's gonna see it? Does the PTA read German magazines?"

"They might. You know, if you look up close, you can see through—"

"I know, I know."

Somebody picked up another phone in the house. "I made a naked picture once."

"Abuela, you did not."

"But that was before the aquanet. Now you will be in the computer with your *tetas* showing. I told you. Nobody listens to me."

"*Mamá, por favor!*" Mom shouted. I could hear Sabrina laughing.

"They're not showing," I said. "I'm wearing a bra."

Robby shouted, "What are *tetas*?"

"Here's your father," said Mom. "He's very upset."

"I'm very upset, Allee," said Dad. "What are those goddamn people in Miami thinking? You're seventeen years old, for the love of God. It's completely inappropriate!" he yelled.

"It's high fashion!" I screamed back, really pissed now. They just didn't get it. "I was *lucky* to get that job. Lucky!" And then I repeated something I heard Claudette say once. "Appropriateness is highly overrated."

"What the hell are you talking about? Have you looked at this picture up close? You can see—"

"Then don't look!" I shrieked. "And tell Mom she won't have to worry about me embarrassing her again. I'm going to Japan!" I slammed down the phone.

I really wasn't going to Japan. I mean, I'd just said that to freak him out because I was so mad. I hadn't decided what I was doing.

Dad called back an hour later. I was on the futon eating Oreos and milk, a treat I hadn't had in months, and looking through my portfolio when the phone rang. "Hello."

"Hi, Allee."

"Hi, Dad."

"Are you really going to Japan?" I guess he was done ranting about the lingerie picture. "I called Monique. She told me about it."

"I don't know."

He sighed. "It's just not practical, Allee. You're not going to model for the rest of your life, are you? Modeling was just a way to get that extra lump sum in the bank to finance your education. You're forgetting that."

"So you think I should just go to college. Not even consider it."

"What will come of it, Allee? You can always go to Japan on a vacation. Come home, finish high school, and go to college. You have a brilliant mind. Don't waste it."

"You just want me to stop modeling because of the whole lingerie editorial."

"That's true, yes. I think you've forgotten who you are. It will be easier for your mother and me if we know you're not modeling anymore. We'd like you to come home for summer school and then go to college."

So that was it. He was making the decision for me. I was about to hang up when suddenly, I remembered what the March Hare told Alice: *Say what you mean and mean what you say.*

"Look, Dad, this isn't about you and Mom. I have a big decision to make, and it shouldn't be about how you and Mom feel. "

Seconds ticked by. I was trembling a little. It wasn't easy being assertive with the people you're closest to.

He sighed again. "I know that, I know. But why did you do that lingerie picture? I thought you were against women being portrayed that way. You look . . . you look . . ."

"Like a model, Dad. Because that's what I am. You were all supportive of me being a model back in January."

"I never thought you'd do a picture like that. You can't tell me you were comfortable being photographed like that."

"No, I wasn't. I should have asked more questions about the booking, taken more control of what I was getting myself into. I know that now. But I didn't know it then." I paused to see if he said anything. He didn't. I looked down at my portfolio, at all the interesting and beautiful photos. "The thing is, Dad, I kinda like modeling. A lot more than I thought I would, you know? And maybe in the future, when I'm older, I might even feel comfortable doing a lingerie shoot, who knows?" I checked to see if he

241

was still there. He cleared his throat, so I added, "It's something I have to figure out for myself."

"So what are you saying? You're saying you're going to Japan instead of *Yale*? Is that what you're saying?"

"I don't know where I'm going right now."

"Oh. Great."

"Does Mom want to talk to me?"

"She's taking a nap."

"Oh. Okay, well, I guess I'll say good-bye then."

"Okay, bye. No, wait. Don't hang up."

"Why?"

"I just wanted to say that, uh, I love you. No matter what you decide to do, your mother and I will always love you."

"I love you too, Dad."

Running always helped me figure things out. I didn't know if it was the breathing getting more oxygen to my brain or what. It could have been what I was listening to that got my synapses connecting (Green Day, Linkin Park, Brainless Wankers) but after about forty minutes of beach jogging, everything was clearer.

I was still reeling from the phone calls. I couldn't believe what Dad had said. I hadn't forgotten who I was. Modeling may have opened my eyes, but it didn't change the real me. I mean, I still loved to read and run and tease my sister. I still wanted to get a Ph.D. someday. He thought I'd turned into some crazy lingerie-posing party animal or something.

The partying in the model world was one of the "cons" I'd been thinking about, trying to decide what to do. I didn't love being surrounded by drinking and smoking every night. And as for the drugs, forget it. They weren't for me. But then again, there would be all of that in college too, even at Yale.

And a part of me wondered if I was really ready for the routine life of school. Modeling had kinda set me free from routines, made me relax more. And modeling had taught me a lot about myself. I didn't feel so closed off from people anymore. That fly-on-the-wall feeling was gone. Modeling tapped into a side of me I hadn't known was there.

It brought out the Alice side of me, the adventurous, playful side. And I wanted to know that part of me better. Maybe the best way to do that was to keep exploring new things. Starting with Japan.

But I wanted the college life, the discussions about great books, the great professors. I wanted to be around people who got what I was talking about, who loved working out their brain, not just their body.

Although I could get an education in Japan too, one I'd never get at any university. There were tons of cultural sights in Japan. I could travel, take Japanese, maybe.

I'd always done what my parents wanted, what was expected of me, followed the rules. I was nothing like the strong young women in all those books I read. I'd never stood up for myself. Not really.

But then again, maybe there was no reason to fight them this time. Maybe they were right about going straight to college.

I'd always thought I was this big thinker, but this was the first time I'd ever really had to think for myself about my own life and what I should do with it.

And so I made my decision.

· · ·

The post office at Thirteenth and Washington was an architectural landmark. It was built in the thirties and had a really dramatic entrance, a huge domed rotunda.

It was as huge as the decision I'd just made.

I took a last look at the envelope addressed to Yale. Last night, I'd stared at those two boxes for an hour, one labeled WILL ATTEND and one labeled WILL NOT ATTEND.

And then I'd checked the box that was best for me.

What will become of me?

chapter (23)

I hadn't told anyone where I was going yet. I didn't want to hear any more opinions about what I should do, so I'd only told my family. Now I wanted to take one last drive around South Beach before I had to hit the highway. Brynn and Claudette helped me pack, but I had a lot more clothing now, so I had to go out and buy another suitcase. Claudette kept playing with my hair, squeezing my shoulders. Brynn didn't say much, just wisecracks, as usual. Her eyes were red and not because we were out all night. She was soft under that hard shell. I knew she would rather be wasted or high than feel deep emotions. She was high now. I could tell by the way she was sniffing and twitching. What would happen to her?

We started the big huggy-kissy good-bye at the car. Claudette said, "Be brave, babygirl, like me. I'll e-mail you from Milan."

"You better. Where are you going, Brynn?"

"Not sure yet."

"Call me. Or e-mail."

"I will." She wouldn't. I hugged her tight. And it wasn't awkward this time. "Luca's coming soon. I better get ready. You take care, Allee."

"I will."

After she went inside, Claudette said, "The agency dropped her yesterday. She didn't want you to know."

I shouldn't have been surprised, but I was. I let out a big *whoosh* of air. "Maybe it's for the best. She needs some time to clean herself up."

"Yeah."

"You did call her mom, right? Because that's the only person she'll listen to."

"Yeah, she'll be here by tonight. She's gonna take Brynn home, get her in a program. Did you know Brynn's real name is Brenda?"

I shook my head no. "Luca will be devastated."

"He supplies the drugs. She needs to get away from him."

"He may love her, but he's not good for her," I agreed.

"Sure you can't stay a few more hours? The World Erotic Art Museum on Twelfth and Washington is having a naughty pastry exhibit and tasting."

"I wouldn't eat anything there if I were you."

Claudette threw her head back and belly-laughed. She grabbed my hands, squeezed them. Then her face got serious.

"Don't do it, Allee. Don't go to Japan. I've always wanted to go back to college, but I'm caught up in the business now. If you don't go to school in the fall, you never will."

"I don't know if that's—"

"You never will. You'll get sucked into the business and you'll never go back. Trust me." It seemed so defeatist. I thought Claudette was all for living on the edge and everything. I guess not going back to college was her greatest regret in life. She gave my hands one last squeeze, then hugged me for a long time. Finally, she blew me a kiss and went back inside to pack for her flight tonight.

I waited for Miguel, who arrived at the center of a Roller-blading cyclone. Trying to pass other bladers on a narrow sidewalk never ended well. He wiped out and landed on the grass. I reached out and helped him up in his little red shorts and knee pads. What a cutie.

Miguel took in my backseat full of luggage, the plastic bags of clothing. "You're making a mistake, Allee Cat. Why even bother going back to Cape Caca? Tell your parents to mail your stuff to Agence and don't look back."

"Miguel, I never said I was going home."

"So you're going to Japan?" He was ready to turn a cartwheel.

"I never said that either."

"I just don't understand. Why go back to who you were when you could be so much more?" Miguel thought the modeling world was the epicenter of the universe. It was completely beyond him that someone would choose to leave it.

I had prepared a speech for him. "I'll miss you a lot. You were always there for me, and you got me to laugh when I was more depressed than I've ever been. You brought out all the good things that were bottled up inside me, opened up a whole new world to me, taught me so much. I can't thank you enough for everything."

It choked him up. He made a fist and tapped his chest. "What are you going to do without me?"

chapter 24

My Beetle picks up speed as I switch to the center lane. I have to make sure I don't miss my exit, 836 WEST, to the airport. I've got a plane to catch.

To Tokyo.

It was easy to make my decision once I remembered what the Cheshire cat told Alice. She asked him, "Would you tell me, please, which way I ought to go from here?" And the cat answered, "That depends a good deal on where you want to get to."

Easy answer.

Wonderland.

There's more than one, you know.